# OFF THE ICE

Chesterford Coyotes 1

_____

RJ SCOTT

V.L. LOCEY

Love Lane Books

# Copyright

# Off the Ice

**A coming-of-age love story with high school, hockey rivalry, friendship, family, and coming out.**

Soren's world changes in an instant when he and his younger brother are adopted by hockey royalty. Making sense of his new life is hard enough, but when he's enrolled in a private school it means facing a whole new set of problems. Navigating friendship, family, and hockey is one thing, but being attracted to the boy who vexes him is a whole new level.

Felix has a reputation to protect. He's the kid who seems to have everything but looks can be deceiving. Spinning lies about his perfect life, he's created a fantasy world that even he has started to believe. Only, it's not long before everything crumbles, all of his pretty lies are revealed, and only his closest rival sees through his pain and stands by him.

Fighting is easy, friendship is hard, but love is everything.

## Dedication

*To my family who accepts me and all my foibles and quirks. Even the plastic banana in my holster.*
*VL Locey*

---

*Always for my family.*
*RJ Scott*

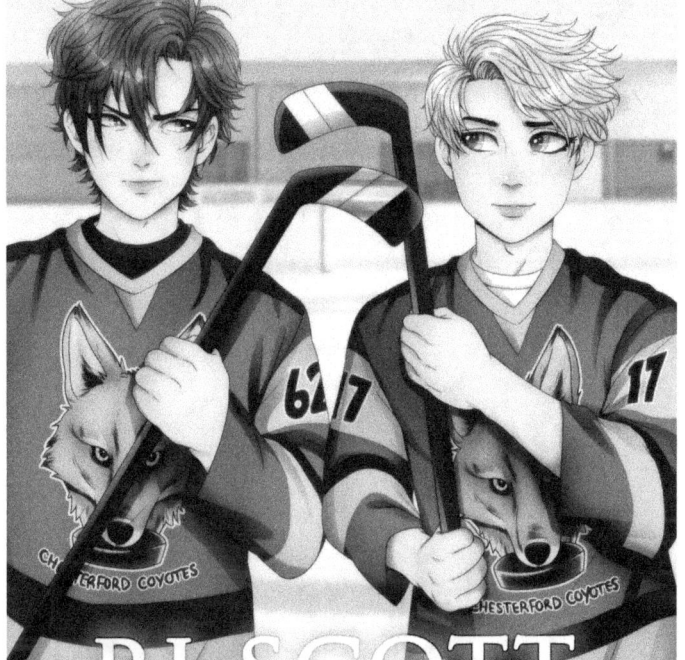

# OFF THE ICE

## CHESTERFORD COYOTES 1

# RJ SCOTT
# V.L. LOCEY

## Chapter One

### Soren

"… A GOOD SUMMER WHERE YOU ENJOYED yourselves and, yet, practiced and worked out as much as possible. Welcome to the JV Hockey squad, which is a responsibility to not only yourself, but to your family and, perhaps biggest of all, to Chesterford Academy."

Coach Sennett paused as he scanned the room. I'd heard a similar speech to this last year, only then, it had been me as a newbie, unsure of my place in the world, let alone the team.

"Remember that what you accomplish on the ice, here, follows you through the rest of your lives. What you strive for academically, also will. We've lost some of our seniors, but we've picked up some new faces, and we'll work hard to come together as a team first, then, we'll click as the champions I know we can be. Go Coyotes!"

"Go Coyotes!"

We all shouted and clapped for Coach's speech. Everyone respected our coach because he was a good guy, warm and open to all his players. He'd played in the AHL for seventeen years, then took this position after he retired, and his word was law.

When he and the other coaches—both volunteers —as well as Mr. Holley, our hockey director, left the locker room, we all looked at each other. Coach was right, there *were* new faces. Some freshmen who'd managed to fill the open slots on the team, but there were more sophomores—like me—and it was on the older guys to help the younger ones.

Shaun Stanton stood up and addressed the room from the lofty position of being the best player on the team from last year. "Okay, Connor Clooney, our previous captain, is now on the varsity team, so we're going to need to think and vote on a new captain. Voting will run through the next two weeks, so think hard on who you feel will fill the role best." He smiled at the newbies. "I know you freshmen don't know us well, but we're all amazing, smart, and incredibly handsome." We all chuckled. It was obviously true, but we all knew we'd be voting to make Shaun our new captain. "You'll get to know us better over the course of our practices leading up to the season opener against the Altoona Hawks."

We all booed at the name of one of our competitors. The freshmen joined in, and we were already bonding. Coach would be so proud. Smiling at the bullshit Shaun was tossing out, I scanned the room, happy to be back for another season. I enjoyed the sport, and while some people thought I was for sure aiming to be a pro player, given one of my adoptive fathers —Tennant Madsen-Rowe—was a generational phenom and skated for the Harrisburg Railers; not to mention my other dad—Jared Madsen-Rowe—was a coach for the Railers and played at the NHL level; I wasn't sure that was what I wanted to do with my life.

I really enjoyed working with kids, so maybe a counselor? I knew what it was like to come up through the system before being lucky enough to get adopted. Still, I had time to figure it out. As my one dad, Jared, said: "There's no need to decide your entire future before you can even drive." Not that driving was that far off. I'd be sixteen in October.

My adoptive parents are cool. Jared is cool. So is Ten. I couldn't have asked for better fathers for me and Milo. I couldn't be luckier.

Raucous laughter came from the far corner where Felix Maxwell-Sinclair held court. Ugh. That dude was a complete dick, and the only person from last year's team that I detested. I wasn't sure how he could skate, what with that fat head and that stick shoved so far up his ass. I mean, sure, he was cute, hot even, but man… those looks did not make up for his toilet personality. Richest kid on campus, he had two lumbering dumb-ass suck-ups who followed him everywhere, and who laughed loudly at whatever Felix said. Given the way the ass was staring at the back of my friend Tyler's head, I bet he'd said something nasty.

Tyler—my fellow winger—was jawing about something, and then, he turned to face Felix, saying something. Felix was wearing that sneer that someday, someone would be jonesing to knock off his face, and I hoped I was there to witness it.

Just as I was thinking of Felix's face meeting a fist, he shot to his feet, gave Tyler a shove, and jumped on the smaller guy when Tyler fell off the bench to the floor. I reacted instantly, and was into the fray in a second, rolling Felix off Tyler with a body check that would have cleared any of the Railers off their skates. Not really, but it sounded boss. Tyler was smaller than most, a speed demon on ice, but we protected him—I protected him.

"Get the fuck off me!" Felix snarled, swinging at me as we grappled for control. He was strong, about my height and weight, but I had the advantage. Or I thought I did. He swung back in a flash, clocking me in the mouth. My front teeth dug into my lower lip, and I tasted blood, which kind of pissed me off. We wrestled around amid shouts from our teammates until I managed to get him under control. Mostly.

He was splayed out on the floor, his face pressed into a pair of wet sneakers lying in front of a locker. I put my knee into his back while the other guys scrambled to get Tyler on his feet.

"What the hell, Sinclair?" I barked down at Felix. We never used our full last names, not since he'd decided that having gay dads meant I didn't deserve to inherit both last names. Whatever. He hated that I responded in kind, and that was just one more point against the freaking idiot.

"Get off my back, Rowe!" he snarled, adding something else to the comment, which was hard to make out since his face was jammed into a skanky, soggy, grey and black Nike belonging to one of the guys who had run here across the sodden sports field. Caleb had kicked them off to wring out his socks but had yet to dress his smelly feet. Caleb liked to hear us complain about his foot stink for some reason. Dude was weird.

It sounded like Felix might have used a queer slur, but I couldn't be sure it was the F-word, although I'd heard him use it before. He should think twice about using that in front of me. My new family was all kinds of queer, as were I and a few other players. Coach, also, did not put up with any racist, sexist, or queer slurs. I'd already hit Felix once, way back, when he started shit about my dads, but that had ended up with me in an office with my new dads, wondering if they were going to send me back in the system.

Of course, they hadn't—they loved me and Milo, and wanted us as their sons, alongside their daughter. We were family, and it was all official and everything. Still, the thought that I'd disappoint my dads meant I genuinely tried not to rise to Felix and hit him again.

But he'd jumped Tyler, and that wasn't right.

I glanced up through my mop of dark hair that really did need cutting, to see Tyler was on his feet, shaking. I swallowed blood, jumping off Felix before stumbling to stand and taking a few steps back to give him room. He pushed to his expensive sneakers, blond hair in his eyes, mud smeared across his cheek and mouth, and glared at me.

"Fuck right off, Rowe!" Felix shouted, then pulled the back of his hand across his face.

"What happened?" One of the team asked.

Tyler began rambling about breakfast cereal and how he hoped his mom had bought milk so he could stuff himself on Count Chocula when he got home, and that he thought Felix might not like cereal. None of that made any sense at all, and I eyed Felix as he spat on the floor, then shoved people aside to stalk out of the locker room, never bothering to explain why he'd jumped Tyler.

"Okay, so Sinclair is obviously not a fan of the deliciousness that is Count Chocula," I said loudly, hoping to deescalate things a bit. A few of the guys snickered. Tyler gave me a look and a shrug. I licked at the split on my lip. Blood still oozed out of it. I wasn't sure how I'd explain a split lip to my father when he picked me up in fifteen minutes, but I was the king of quick thinking. I'd come up with something...

---

"OKAY, SO YOU WANT TO RUN THAT PAST ME AGAIN?" Dad asked as I buckled into the passenger seat. Milo was in the back, brown eyes wide, staring at me openly. He also went to Chesterford Academy, but the elementary school building was on the other side of the large green grounds.

"I tripped going into homeroom," I said, peeking into the backseat at my ten-year-old brother. His eyes were round as hubcaps. "I'm a dork."

"Your feet are too big," Milo said, his worry seeming to disappear after I gave him a lopsided smile.

It hurt to smile, but for him I would. Then, I leaned around the seat even more to wink at my little sister, Lottie. Charlotte had started kindergarten this year and was in her car seat reading. The girl read a lot. Like all the time. Simple words mostly, but she was growing her vocabulary daily. She was always coming to me to read big books to her, and we spent hours curled up with fantasy novels—me, her, Milo, and our dog, Gordie, on the couch in the playroom reading about dragons, heroes and heroines, and mystical palaces floating in the clouds.

"Your feet smell," Charlotte told me. I stuck out my tongue, and she giggled.

"Soren, your lip?" Dad asked, pulling me back to the puffy lip and outright lie I'd decided to tell. It kind of sat badly on my tongue. Or maybe that was the rank taste of old blood. No, it was the lie. Totally. I undid my tie with a sigh.

"Tripped. I was looking at Chelsea Myers' new sweater and—"

"Right, we don't need to go into more detail," Jared said, rolling his eyes to the back seat.

"Why did she get a new sweater?" Milo asked as he tried to dig something out from under his booster seat.

"Is it pink?" Lottie inquired from behind me. She was into pink. This week. Last week it was purple. The week before red. Which was why everyone in the house got new mani/pedis every week. All three of us wore Chesterford uniforms in red, black, and blue, our school colors. Lottie's was a little pleated skirt in dark blue, while Milo and I wore slacks. Sexist much, board members? Like, are we in the fifties or what?

"No, it was white and fluffy," I replied, Jared

giving me a look. "Chelsea has really nice... sweaters."

"Mm-hmm," Jared mumbled as we waited for the kids in front of us to pile into their cars. "It's nice to know that the young lady has attractive clothing."

Jared was bi, like me, so he got the whole pretty girls in sweaters thing. So did his son—my half-brother now—Ryker, NHL skater who was also bi, but married to a gay guy. Like Jared was to Ten. As I said, our house was queer from floor to rafter.

"Yep, really nice sweaters." I smiled at the mental image of Chelsea. Yeah, she had *incredibly* nice sweaters.

"Try to keep your eyes on where your feet are taking you instead of sweaters next time," Jared said, easing away from the curb to follow a gold SUV away from the drop-off and pick-up point at the front of the administration building. The school buses Chesterford provided to students within a certain radius of the school had already left for the day. I'd been a little late for pickup due to hockey practice, or hockey-hello-again day I guess it would be called. "How was the welcome back to the Coyotes meeting?"

"Oh, cool. Yeah, it was tight."

"Tight. Good. Well, as long as it was tight." Dad

smiled at me, then turned out of the circular driveway to head back to Harrisburg and home. I already had homework. The first day of school, and the teachers were nailing us with work. I mean yeah, I was an honors student, but did we have to jump into calculus on day one? No, no we didn't. It sucked. Kind of like Felix Maxwell-Sinclair. Maybe Felix sucked more. It was too close to call, to be honest.

## Chapter Two

### Felix

SOREN ROWE COULD SUCK A BAG OF DICKS.

People were looking at me—talking about me and passing judgment, and it was all Soren's fault.

So I'd jumped Tyler—what was it to do with anyone else? Least of all Soren, who'd probably been telling everyone how he pushed me to the ground and shoved my face in a sneaker.

Asshole.

I tilted my chin, ignored everyone staring and talking behind their hands, and decided that, on day two of school, I was already over everyone's shit.

Tyler got what he deserved, thinking he could get away with talking to me as if that was okay. It was bad enough he'd been at *my* house yesterday morning when I woke up—but the fact that his mom had been standing in our kitchen making pancakes and doling out sugary cereal like she was my mom or something, had been a slap in my face. She'd even asked me if I slept okay, and that was a step too far.

Mom had only been gone three months, and I was gutted that Dad had jumped quickly into another relationship—as if his marriage meant nothing. Did he really need to have someone staying over when I'd just gotten used to the silence in the house? Because there he was, inviting a strange woman into our house, and worse, she'd had her freaking kid in tow.

Tyler Corrigan—*the gay one*, with his ridiculous floppy hair and rainbow pins—had this way of trying to talk to me just because my dad was boning his mom, as if I even cared he was breathing. Fuck that shit. I didn't want or need anyone messing with my mornings, or coming up to me and chatting about types of breakfast cereal, all while his mom was visiting *my* house with *my* dad.

There was no faint glimmer of hope that, maybe, one day, Mom would come back, and we'd be a nuclear freaking family, because she'd managed to forget I was her *son*, but that was a thought for another day. The divorce wasn't even final yet, and even though I never wanted them in the same place again because the fights were insane, that didn't mean Dad could force another kid onto me in my own home.

Miles and Jonah closed in around me—my barrier against the whispers—and I tensed when Miles chuckled.

"I heard you hit Tyler yesterday, and it was some funny shit," Miles smirked at my side. "Someone in homeroom said you went headfirst into a sneaker—"

I shot him a look, and he subsided immediately, shrunk down from his six feet to become nothing at all next to me. He might be built like an ox—a football defenseman—and had a string of hot girlfriends, but *his* dad worked for *my* mom's company, which still had offices back in Harrisburg, and that gave me a unique standing in his life. Same with the other half of the duo who followed me everywhere—Jonah—whose aunt also worked for my mom, and it was because of that connection that he was even at this school. They weren't friends, unless I said so, and they owed me and my family, both of them. The last thing I needed was for one of them to throw smartass comments around on the subject of me falling on my ass.

Money calls to money, and Miles was an idiot, but

if he and Jonah kept quiet, and backed me up on anything I did or said, then they served a purpose. I didn't want or need people to hang out with, so they were quite useful as a front. I needed friends about as much as I needed Soren Madsen-Rowe getting in the middle of a fight between me and Tyler, when Tyler had it coming. My hand still ached from where it connected with Soren's jaw, but the satisfying feeling of hitting him was worth every ache I'd woken up with.

*I think.*

"Maybe Soren is the one you need to talk to," Jonah said bravely, after I'd warned Miles to shut up with just a glare. Soren was the one person in this school who didn't seem to give a shit who my dad was, or whether or not I could buy and sell Soren's new dads five times over. He confronted me at every given opportunity, faced me down in the hallways, hip-checked me on the ice, and worst of all, he reveled in all of it, with his huge dark eyes and his expressive smile, and his, also ridiculous, wavy hair flying this way and that.

Had he not heard of product?

Soren may well have lucked out with his adoption, landing a pity placing with NHL star Tennant Madsen-Rowe and his husband, but he didn't have style, or ambition, or money. He'd been nothing to start with, and he'd end up being nothing, but still, he got under my skin, and yesterday morning's shitfest was no exception. He'd pulled me off Tyler, all up in my face, breathing on me, messing up my jacket, and worst of all, he'd bested me.

Only because I hadn't seen it coming.

Nothing to do with the fact it had been me who had lost control in the first place.

I spotted Tyler again, over by his locker, scrubbing at his shirt—he'd probably spilled half his lunch down the front as usual—and I headed over with a sharp *"with me"* to Miles and Jonah. I wasn't stupid. I checked around first to see if he was alone, not wanting a repeat of what had happened with the rest of the goddamned hockey team standing in a freaking circle.

I caged Tyler against the locker, amused that he thought to offer me a hesitant smile, and more satisfied that there was a frisson of fear crossing his face. He should fear me, one word to my dad, and his mom would be out of my dad's bed as quick as I could shove him into the boards.

"My dad may well be fucking your mom," I growled low in my throat.

He winced, then seemed to deflate. "He's not—"

"Shut up."

Tyler was a thin kid, wiry, fast on his skates for our team, but I was bigger, and I could break him in an instant if there was no one around to fight for him. "You tell your skanky ass mom that if she dares to bring herself or her trash to our place again, then there'll be trouble."

Tyler mumbled something.

I leaned so close that his breath was on my cheek. "Spit it out," I said.

"He's kind to her," Tyler blurted. "She likes him."

I slammed the flat of my hand against the locker, and it shook, and Tyler's eyes widened.

I turned to leave, Miles falling into line, and Jonah jogging to catch up. I chose to ignore Tyler's soft words, even if I heard them clearly. "She likes him."

After a moment, it seemed Miles was going to break the silence. "What exactly happened with your dad and Tyler's mom—" I rounded on Miles and shoved a finger in his chest.

"Nothing. You heard, *nothing*."

He nodded, and I stared at Jonah, who had a weird expression that soon changed when he caught me looking at him. Then, the three of us carried on to this year's first chem class, the suckiest of classes in a list of suck. At least in chem, I didn't have to worry about

Tyler, or Soren, or any of the kids who didn't back down, because this was the lowest grade of chem, and I had manipulated my way into staying at that level, just because I hated it, and Mr. Anders was an ass who felt he could tell the kids what to do as if we were idiots.

Who even needed chem anyway?

The three of us commandeered the back row, sending one new kid scurrying to the front, and I pulled out my chemistry highlight notes from last year, scanning them quickly.

"Okay, pop quiz!" Mr. Anders announced from the front of the class.

Everyone groaned. He separated the sheets of multiple-choice questions and asked people at the front to pass them back. It gave me time to do one last flick over the notes in my book, and when we turned over the sheet, I filled in just enough correct answers to stay under the magic sixty percent that meant I'd be put up into a class where I'd actually have to work. Didn't matter that I knew all the answers, or that I could probably be in AP Chem if I tried, the same as I was in AP English and Math; I didn't want to be.

When your mom's family founded Sinclair-Staten Pharma it was kind of expected that chemistry would be a skill.

I needed math. I reluctantly needed English. But, again, given I wanted nothing to do with Sinclair-Staten, who needed chem?

Not this billionaire hedge-fund manager-in-training. Not me.

We learned about chemical equations in the lesson —I think—but I spent most of it with my reference book propped on the table, alternating between doodling and staring at my phone, and copying the basic notes from the whiteboard. Stocks in Sinclair-Staten had hit an all-time high—seemed like Mom's side of the family was *this close* to being the newest billionaires on the block. Of course, it was on paper only, but the company was only a few hundred thousand behind Rhianna, and handling money was way more important than music. Money built communities—all music did was suck my time.

The bell sounded, and I was up and out of my seat before we were dismissed, but Mr. Anders blocked the door.

"A moment, Felix," he asked, and everyone streamed past me, including Miles and Jonah when Mr. Anders ushered them out. He closed the door after them all and indicated the closest desk. "Take a seat."

I very deliberately checked my watch—my very

expensive, cost more than the teacher's salary, watch —and then, stifled a pretend yawn before sitting.

Mr. Anders rifled through the pop quizzes and pulled out the one with my name at the top.

"So, you answered correctly that the chemical formula of carbon dioxide is $CO_2$."

"Yep." That was such an easy one that I knew it was safe to answer that, even if it hadn't been in my brief cheat sheet. He inclined his head, and resentment shot through me. "Yes, sir," I muttered, with as little respect as I could muster.

He raised a single eyebrow. "And then, a little further down, you answered about the critical point pressure of water."

All I heard was the word water, and yep, $H_2O$ was another of the easy questions I'd be expected to know at this level. "Yes, sir."

"You remember choosing that answer?"

"Yes, sir."

"For real, you studied, and you chose the correct answer with your extensive knowledge of water."

"Yes, sir." Where was this leading?

"One of the hardest questions on the pop quiz, and that wasn't a guess?"

Fuck. Wait. What? Had I messed up and answered one of the harder questions correctly?

He nodded; his expression inscrutable. "And yet, the next question about the chemical formula of water, possibly the easiest, you got very wrong."

I thought on my feet. "I guessed at the answers," I lied, and began to dig a hole for myself.

He huffed a laugh. "All of them?"

"All of them."

He considered me for a moment, his beady teacher eyes staring right through me. "I'm recommending you're moved up a class."

I sat up in my seat. "You're what now?"

"You no more need remedial support than I need your staring-out-of-the-window attitude in my class," he summarized and waited for me to answer.

All I wanted to do was lash out—having to attend science classes and actually having to work was like a slap to the face, but also, it scared me, and I hated that feeling. I might have a semi-photographic memory, but to have to work at something I hated and didn't need, and maybe fail?

Maxwell-Sinclair men didn't fail.

"My mom donated money for the science block, you know," I tried a little desperately.

"And you're not using it enough," Mr. Anders responded as fast. Damn him.

My chest tightened, my heartbeat quickened, and

emotion clouded my thoughts. He was staring at me as if he expected me to fight, and I knew he wouldn't back down, so I'd save my fight for another day. "If that's all?" I asked with considered politeness.

"It is. You'll find your new class details in your online files. There will be studying that you need to complete to get up to scratch, but it's a new year, and you have a fresh start."

I had my fingers around the door handle, and I'd almost escaped, but clearly, he had something else he wanted to poke at me.

"You know something? You could be brilliant at everything if you cared enough," he said.

I bristled, but I didn't stop to answer, just walked outside, and closed the door behind me.

I was already brilliant—I was *born* to shine.

Soren passed by me as I stood immobile, his group of friends around him—a gang of them, as opposed to me with my two wingmen, who had waited for me outside. They were milling about talking loudly about some hockey charity thing. Despite being on the hockey team, I hadn't heard about it, so I guess it was something to do with Soren's two new dads.

Not that I cared.

Soren caught my gaze, shook his head a little as if

he were disappointed that he saw me or something, and I couldn't fail to see the way Tyler moved to hide behind him, and how Soren put his arm over Tyler's shoulder, as if he didn't care people would see him hugging the flighty kid with the pink hair.

Almost as if they were real friends.

## Chapter Three

### Soren

"Okay, so what exactly is Felix's perpetual problem?" Courtney asked as we made our way to AP Chinese class. I shrugged. My best friend rolled her eyes before giving her grape gum a loud crack. Tyler literally jumped. The poor guy was not the bravest lion in the pride, but he was trying to be, and that was what counted. "That kid has no personality other than uptight asshole in an elitist school uniform."

"We all wear elitist school uniforms," I reminded her as we left Tyler at his trig class, then moved to the languages wing of the high school, saying goodbye to Asher at the Spanish classroom.

"I know, but we take them off when we get home.

He probably wears the Chesterford colors to bed. Probably spanks off as he dreams of old Alistair Chesterford in his powdered wig and buckled shoes."

That comment made me snort. "He takes the uniform off at night." She gave me a look. "No, I don't know that personally, not like I've ever seen him in bed or anything."

"I should hope not," she tossed out as we entered class.

We slid into our seats near the front, by the windows. I always took the window seats. I liked having the sun on the side of my face while being able to peep at nature. I'd not realized how much I enjoyed being outdoors until the adoption. Now, we had a huge yard to play around in and went on camping trips during the summer. I was going to kind of hate it when training camp opened for our dads in October. They'd be traveling all the time then, and we'd have our grandparents taking care of us. Not that I disliked Ten's parents. I loved them. They were as cool as people that old could be.

"Please, like I would ever." I pulled my textbook out as Court began prattling on about field hockey and how she wished their first game wasn't against Carlisle, as she had dated one of the girls on that team last year for like five days. Dana? Doris? Daisy? I couldn't recall. Courtney liked to play the field. Field. Hockey. Yuk. Field hockey pun for the win.

Ms. Chen walked into the class, smiling at her returning students. Being in AP Chinese was not an easy task. Generally, the first-year class was reserved for seniors to ready them for college language courses. I had a knack for languages, though, and Courtney was half-Chinese on her mother's side, her dad was an NBA player, which was where she got her dark skin and long legs. Also, her gift for talking. Her dad could talk the ears off a brass monkey as my grandfather liked to say. She spoke Mandarin at home, so this course was a piece of cake for her and kept her GPA up with the rest of us honor society brats.

As we dove into our first assignment—reading the front page of a newspaper from Shanghai to refresh what we had learned last year—I fell into the story about a man and a cat, my Mandarin was a little rusty from not having been used all summer, but still intact. For the most part. Court helped me where I got stuck as she snuck peeks at her phone.

"I'm going to hit on Brice soon." My bestie whispered.

I glanced down at her lap. Oh, okay, Brice. From the basketball team. Yeah, I'd hit on him, too, if he weren't straight and already heavy on the trail of some girl named Bianca, who was the head of the fashion club. Yeah, we had all kinds of clubs here that were not sport-related. Chess, fashion, school paper, gamer—which I was a member of—cooking, film, photography, Queer Alliance, of which I was also a member, plus a few hundred other clubs. Chesterford liked extracurricular activities. A lot. They built leadership skills according to my counselor. They'd also look good on the college applications that we'd all be sending out in a year or two.

"I thought he was sniffing around Bianca," I replied on the sly, my gaze darting to Ms. Chen at her desk. She was an older woman with dark eyes and hair cut into a bob. She always wore flowery dresses with a belt.

"Yeah, he is, but she's not interested in him. She's hot for Duante, that guy with the red hair on the baseball team?" I shook my head and tried to focus on the words in front of me. "You know who I mean."

"No, I don't. What is this word?" I tapped at the crumpled newspaper on my desk.

"Shipbuilder," she said after giving the paper a cursory glance. "Duante is that redhead on the baseball team. Slim, tall, likes to wear those tropical bucket hats all the time."

"Oh, okay, yeah I know who you mean. So, this says that the shipbuilder found his cat under a whale?"

"What? Let me see." She spun my page around, then giggled softly. "Dope. No, like really, would the cat be under a whale? You're such a loser. That word is wharf. See?"

Right, yeah, that rang true. "Thanks. Hey, are you still planning on joining me for that live stream of *Knights of the Green Helm* tonight at eight?"

"I'll for sure play with you. I have to make sure I get my homework done first, though, so don't be texting me all afternoon like you do."

"*Me*? Girl, you are confused. It's you texting *me* about rando people you want to hook up with."

She had the grace to blush, but only a little. "Life is short, Soren. Why not enjoy it while we can? We'll be all withered up and in our thirties before we know it."

"True."

"Mr. Madsen-Rowe and Ms. Dunn." We both fell silent when Ms. Chen called our names. Then proceeded to ask us, in Mandarin, if we were talking about the newspaper article, to which we said *yes*, because mostly, we had been. "Good," Ms. Chen said, in English. "Then, you won't mind standing and reading your articles to the class."

Yep, second day in, and I'd already been called out. Looked like this year was off to a hella good start.

---

I'D CALLED IT.

In AP Chinese, I'd predicted things would tumble into the shit tank, and I'd been right. Go Soren. Woot.

Today's third period chemistry found me staring at the back of Felix Sinclair's fat, bougie head. Like having him in AP English after lunch wasn't bad enough, but now, he was in chem class too? What had I done to deserve this? Had I stepped on an anthill while running across the quad to get to homeroom on time? Had past life Soren committed some kind of foul murderous rampage through London, and I was now paying the price by having to deal with this jerk for two classes, as well as hockey?

Thankfully, Felix didn't turn around to stare at me like he always did, as if I were a pile of cat puke he'd stepped in. When the bell rang, he bolted out of class to meet up with his sidekicks Jerk and Off in the hallway. I ignored them all as I made my way to the next class, their stupid comments about my parentage only pissing me off slightly. Everyone here knew my and Milo's story. Poor kids in the system adopted by hockey royalty. Plucked from the dumpster by sports stars, dressed up in fine clothes and sent to the most prestigious private school in the greater Harrisburg area.

"I can smell the trailer park on him still," Felix liked to call after me whenever there wasn't an adult around to hear him. The coward. I'd lived in a trailer park, sure. I'd lived just about everywhere as a kid, and yeah, I'd worn used clothes from Goodwill and ate government cheese. So what?

Lunch was a lone bright spot as I joined the hockey team to eat—minus Felix of course, who never ate with us. Courtney was there, along with some of the girls' field hockey team, and we all had a few laughs and some pretty good grub. The perks of private school were quality education and the food. Seriously, the munch here was incredible. No one who attended Chesterford went hungry like Milo and I had a few times in our past. Today was whole wheat spaghetti with vegan meatballs, arugula salad with parmesan cheese, cranberry almond slaw, a wheat bun, and milk or juice. Dessert was a cinnamon baked pear.

Sometimes, I had to remind myself that this was my life now.

The pear and the company helped wash away the Felix-in-chem-class taste. It had been hell sitting there behind him smelling that coconut/spice body wash/shampoo/cologne he bathed in.

I hoisted my backpack onto one shoulder as I stood. "Make sure you join us for the stream tonight, okay?" I asked everyone at the table. The cafeteria was loud, sunny, and filled with teenagers making eyes at each other. "If you can't linger, then just lurk okay? We're hoping to pull in some new views to get us over a thousand subs, so tell your friends, right?"

They all said they'd watch or have it on in the background while they studied. I fist-bumped my way down the table, stopping to do a double bestie bump with Courtney before jogging upstairs to the English Department wing. AP English was taught by Mr. Russell, a dude who'd been alive when Shakespeare was penning sonnets. No shit, Mr. Russell was ancient. Nice, but man, was he old. Sometimes, he nodded off in class, then would snort/snore himself awake. Which made for a pretty-laid back class.

Last year, I'd aced the class with minimal effort, so I was all sorts of ready to slide through it again. Only, when I walked into room 312, I found myself staring at someone who was not Mr. Russell. This guy was younger, which, come on, wasn't hard to do, but he smiled at me as I skidded to a halt in the doorway.

"You're in the right class. I'm Mr. Russell." I blinked, then glanced back to see if I had come through some sort of *Dr. Who* time warp portal thing. Nope, same old hall with students rushing past and posters on the walls for upcoming games and dances. "The older Mr. Russell is my father, and he retired over the summer. I'm his replacement. So, please, come in, have a seat, and tell me your name."

"Uhm. Soren Madsen-Rowe," I stammered as I glanced from the happy man in the sweater vest—yep he was related to old Mr. Russell for sure—and found one empty desk. Right next to Felix Maxwell-Sinclair. I got the dark look from Felix as if he were daring me to sit beside him. So, I plunked my ass down in the desk to his left and gave him my biggest grin. He flipped me off in secret.

The bell rang. Mr. Russell closed the door, then turned to face us. His glasses had smears on the lenses, but that didn't seem to bother him.

"Wonderful. What a lovely group of happy faces we have here!" Mr. Russell exclaimed joyfully.

"Oh, for shit's sake, he's a perky one. God save

me from perky teachers," Felix mumbled under his breath.

I had to agree. Perky teachers were just too... perky. I mean if this were Milo's class sure, or Lottie's kindergarten class, sure. But sophomore AP English? Dude, just no.

"I know, it's a new year, and you have a new teacher to contend with, but don't worry. I have all kinds of fun projects lined up for us for the year as I outlined in the online syllabus. You all did read that over, right?"

The entire class muttered in the affirmative, but I would bet my gaming computer that not one kid in here had read that information. I know I hadn't.

"Perfect! Then, we'll dive right into our first assignment. As you saw in the syllabus, we're going to create our own magazines!" Mr. Russell was so excited I thought he might combust. Some of the other students clapped. "I've put you all into pairs for this project. I want your magazines completed and ready for the class to read by Halloween. You can find all the specific details online, so you can reference the page totals and formatting. I know you're all super creative, so wow me with your magazines. Please have your outline to me by next Monday. And no, you cannot create anything pornographic or offensive. Perhaps you can make a travel magazine, or a fashion magazine! Or if you're into sports, you could do an athletic magazine with interviews of our fabulous Chesterford teams and coaches! The sky's the limit."

"Can we do a swimsuit issue?" Pete Murkowski asked, and Mr. Russell turned a shade of red I'd only seen on a beet. "I mean, *Sports Illustrated* does them."

"No, no swimsuit issues," Mr. Russell coughed out. "Now, when I call your name, please go sit with your new partner. Belinda Hayes and Lucy Marlow. Peter Murkowski and Gwendolyn Marks-Lloyd..."

I sat back in my seat, a creeping feeling of dread settling on me as students were paired off with speed. When it was only me and Felix left, I, for serious, groaned out loud when our names were called out as a creative duo.

"And that's the capper on a truly shitty day," Felix huffed.

The world must be spinning to its end. That was twice in one day that I agreed with something Felix "The Snob" Sinclair had said.

## Chapter Four

### Felix

"WE NEED TO TALK ABOUT WHAT WE'RE GOING TO do," Soren said after we'd sat silent for what seemed like forever, but was probably only a few seconds. There was no way I was breaking the silence we had going on, because I had no idea what to say. I glanced at my watch; ten minutes left in this godforsaken excuse for an English class. Mr. Russell, as bouncy as a puppy, had hovered with us, talked at us about inspiration and teamwork and ideas. He wanted at least one pair to focus on the school, because apparently it has a really-super-exciting-challenging history. No one had taken him up on it yet, and there was no way it would be me and *Soren.*

Talking of *him*, he'd been the one to talk first, but all he'd said is that somehow we needed to talk.

"No shit, Sherlock," I muttered.

He sat back, leveled a stare at me that might have broken lesser men, but I was a Maxwell-Sinclair, and we didn't back down from anything. Not even a pauper pretending to be a prince. So, I stared back and checked my watch again. Eight minutes now.

"Wow," Soren breathed and leaned toward me. "Oh my god!" He clapped his hand to his mouth, and his loud exclamation had people looking at us. "Is that a really expensive watch?" he made an *O* with his mouth, as if he was in awe, but I could see it didn't reach his eyes, and I knew for sure, he was trying to press a button.

"The fuck?" I asked, shorthand for leave-me-alone-asshole-we've-only-got-eight-minutes-left.

He held out his hand, made a deliberate show of pulling back his shirt sleeve and acting like he was checking his cheap-as-shit watch, holding his wrist this way and that as if it were encrusted with the crown jewels or something. "Look at me everyone, checking the time on my obscenely expensive watch." He did some more rotations, dropped his hand to the desk, then checked the watch again. "Oh, look it's a minute later!"

Somebody sniggered, and I glared in their general direction in case it was someone who should be cowed by who I am. It was only Pete Murkowski, but he should know better, and he immediately subsided as I faced Soren and tipped my chin.

"I'm surprised your piece of shit works. Don't batteries usually corrode in dumpsters?" I deadpanned.

Soren glanced at me, and for a second I tensed, because the guy had this way about him, all surface emotion and icy disdain for me, and I thought he might hit me. Instead, he leaned back in his chair, casually pushing his perfect fucking hair from his perfect freaking forehead. "Touché." Then, he underscored his words with a smirk. "So anyway, back to this." He tapped the empty sheet of paper and raised a single eyebrow in question. "And?"

"And what?"

He sighed. "Any ideas?"

"None." I was lying, I had a million ideas, something about poems was front and center, or Shakespeare's sonnets, given this was AP English, but there was no freaking way I was exposing my underbelly to Soren like that.

"Well, the easiest one would to focus on hockey," he suggested. "We could talk about the hockey team here from experience, and maybe interview my dads, or—"

"No." God, it hurt for me to say that—the thought of interviewing his dads, particularly Tennant Madsen-Rowe, or indeed any of the Harrisburg Railers, sent a curl of excitement through me. Still, the idea of Soren having something to lord over me was abhorrent.

"Then what?" he said with a sigh.

"Let's talk about hedge-fund management, and we could interview someone with real money, not half-assed *sports dudes*." I wanted to interview someone with a shit ton of money so I could learn how to be them—be better than them—and no excuses from me for feeling that way because being untouchable and rich, making more money, driving a faster car, shit, having a family that stayed together, were life goals that spurred me on.

Soren's lips thinned at the sports/dudes comment. "Hockey is cool."

"Money is cool."

"Spoken like a rich-kid asshole," Soren muttered.

"Jealous?" I parried.

He rolled his eyes. "Of you?" Soren scanned me from my head down to my waist and back up again, and curled his lip. "Hardly."

I bristled. People *were* jealous of me, so why was he so different? I had *everything* compared to so many, and I expected people to envy me. Why was Soren so determined to not show any respect or envy? I ignored the press of confusion and checked my watch again—this time with exaggerated movements —four minutes to go.

"How's it going?" Mr. Perky-McPerkison stopped by our desks.

"Hockey—"

"Money—"

We spoke at the same time, and our teacher stared at us with a sad expression and lowered his voice. "Shame. Okay, though, if you want to choose something that easy." He sighed with added drama. "Seems like there is no one who is clever enough to take on the history of the school," he sighed. "I guess, I shouldn't expect boys your age to be capable of that level of work."

The fuck? I was capable of anything. I was an AP student in some subjects; my grades were good, apart from chemistry, and *no one* told me I couldn't do something. If that meant focusing on the history of the goddamned school, then you'd better believe I was going to create the best project he'd ever seen, and I'd show him exactly what I could do.

"We'll do it," I said.

Soren shot me a sharp glance. "We will?" he said, his eyes wide.

"Yep." I sat back in my chair with my arms over my chest. "Done deal."

Mr. Russell patted my shoulder and wandered away muttering about school colors.

"You were played," Soren said as he shook his head. "Someone tells you that you can't do something, and you're on it like white on rice."

I considered his statement, wanting to deny the truth of it, but I'd been raised on one challenge after another, and he wasn't lying. So, I went on the defensive because who the hell was Soren to think he saw the real me? "You can't tell me you weren't about to agree to it as well."

He shrugged, "Maybe. Maybe not." Then, he scooted the piece of paper over to me. "You decided though, so you start."

"Start what?" I stared at the blank page.

"Write a title, like, I dunno, *The History of Chesterford Academy*, or something. Underline it, then make some boxes for what we can write about."

"You write it." I shoved the paper back at him and waited for him to scrawl across the top, only he stared at me.

"This is a joint project; you write it." He pushed the paper back at me.

"You suggested the title." I pushed it toward him.

"You committed us to the project." Another shove.

"What are you? Five?" I snapped, and took the paper and a pen, and wrote, in my best penmanship, the title and our names underneath. I added four boxes, and then, glanced up at him expectantly. "And?"

"Ghosts," he said, and I almost wrote it down before I realized he was likely messing with me.

"Fuck you Rowe. If you're not taking this seriously, I'm not getting marked down for having to work with a loser who messes this up for me."

Soren leaned into me. "For real, didn't you hear there's a ghost in the janitor's closet?"

"What?"

"Yeah." He made woo-woo hands and fluttered them around him, then lowered his voice to the point I had to lean in, inhaling the scent of the boy I hated, all citrus and sharp, and so close I could see the flecks of gold in his dark eyes. He really did have pretty eyes, the kind that maybe people would stare into and write poems about. Mine were a perfectly ordinary blue, but his were full of light.

"Sometimes," Soren began in a half whisper, "there's clashing and banging in there, and no sign of the janitor, and I was told that, if it's a full moon, sometimes you can hear the noise all the way down in reception."

"What?" I repeated, half intrigued, and the rest pissed that I was even engaging with him.

He sat back and slapped the table. "You're so easy," he smirked.

I wanted to reach over and punch him right in the center of his huge smirking face. Oh god, I wanted to shove him against a locker and… "You're an asshole."

The bell sounded, and he was up and out of his chair before I'd even moved. "Don't forget to write ghosts down," he called back as he left the room.

A couple of people near him laughed. How many of them had heard all that shit? I was mortified, and I collected my books, pen, and the dreaded paper, and shoved it all into my bag with extreme prejudice. I excelled in this class, not because I needed it to become the person I wanted to be, but because of who I was right now. Stories fascinated me, poems, books, words. They were my comfort when my mom was shouting and my dad was backing down, and the pain in my chest was too much.

But Soren, was a thorn in my side, a mess I couldn't keep contained, and by the time I'd exited the classroom, ignoring Mr. Russell's cheerful goodbye, I had so much temper coiled inside me that my skin felt like it was going to tear open.

The corridor was too hot. I vaguely realized that Miles had fallen into step with me, and when I burst through the door and onto the grass beyond, I kept walking until I reached the gym, and through it to the hockey rink. I threw my bag in my cubby, then went to the break room, and slammed pucks at practice targets until my arms ached. Miles hadn't followed me in here—why would he, it wasn't as if he played hockey—so I took every ounce of anger from people laughing at me, and threw the stick at the wall, and when I was done with that, I kicked the spare bucket of pucks for good measure and left it all scattered on the floor.

What I wouldn't give to be able to get skates on and be out on the ice, throwing down with Soren and making him *hurt*.

No one laughed at Felix Maxwell-Sinclair

Worse, no one made people laugh at me and got away with it.

However pretty their goddamned eyes were.

---

THE PIECE OF PAPER MOCKED ME, LYING THERE ON THE desk in my room, crumpled from where I'd unceremoniously dumped it in my bag, and currently, held down with a Railers mug on one side and a signed hockey puck on the other. I could stare at it all night. After all, there was no one here to stop me. Dad had messaged to say he was away for work, and that he'd left a couple of fifties on the counter in case of emergency. I pocketed the cash to add to my pile, because I might not have an emergency today, but what about tomorrow?

I ignored the bit on my dad's note to say I could call any time.

Whatever.

Phoebe and Rick, housekeeper and handyman respectively, husband and wife, had gone back to their place on the edge of the property after Phoebe had dished up dinner for me on my own at the vast kitchen table, and that meant, I had the run of the house given there was no sign of Tyler or his mom visiting us tonight. Good.

I could do anything. Dance to the loudest music ever, watch movies until three a.m., eat what I wanted from the huge walk-in pantry, or drink all the alcohol in my dad's impressive study, but what was I doing instead? Staring at this stupid piece of paper, which stared right back at me.

"The History of Chesterford Academy," I told my room and sighed. I had many regrets about today, but once the temper subsided, I was mostly pissed at myself that I hadn't gone with hockey as our subject choice. I swiveled my chair to face the far wall of my room, angling my desk light so it shone on the posters there. No one outside of my parents, Phoebe, and Rick, knew how much I loved the Harrisburg Railers hockey team, and their images and logo adorned my walls in a huge collage of blue and white. Off to the right was my homage to one of my favorite players— their goalie, the Russian, Stan Gunnerson-Lyamin— holder of two Vezina trophies, and one of the funniest guys I'd ever heard talk. "Me get bigly goal!" I said to his image and huffed a laugh that I was talking to myself in badly accented Russian.

Then, there was a collection of team photos, a couple of the Stanley Cup—the ultimate prize in the NHL—and several of individual players, like Lockhart and the other Gunnerson-Lyamin, Stan's husband, Erik.

Lastly, I focused on Tennant Madsen-Rowe, and I stared at him for the longest time. He was the only person in my life, other than my dad, who'd influenced me in any way. One of the photos I had showed him sitting at a piano, staring down at the keys with the same intensity he used for scoring goals. He was a winner, a survivor from terrible injury, a phenom, a child star player from a family of winners, who'd grown into one of the sexiest hockey players I'd ever seen. He skated fast; he pulled the Railers along with him; he was an All-Star and a champion, and when he came out, with his now husband at his side, it had been the cause of something growing inside me as strong and fierce as my temper.

I was like Ten.

Sort of like Ten.

I wasn't the best hockey player in the world—I never wanted to be, not when I had a rosy future all mapped out for myself—but I played the piano like he did. Even if I'd been forced to learn as a kid and had resented it at first, I grew to love it in the end, and it was another thing to add to my list of accomplishments that would make me the best hedge-fund manager ever.

So, it wasn't hockey we were connected through. It was that, without asking for it, without wanting the mess of it in my life, and with it serving no purpose at all in my plans, I realized I was gay. I wasn't even bisexual; hell, I didn't even look at girls, so my society-approved wife of the future wouldn't be sharing my bed.

I was gay. Just like my idol.

I was gay and staring at Soren's pretty eyes, and for one brief shining moment, catching the flecks in them, and instead of seeing him as an obnoxious asshole, I wondered if there was maybe more to him.

Until the ghost nonsense he'd thrown at me, anyway.

"No," I said to my posters, and whirling back to my desk, I picked up the paper, screwed it into a ball, and threw it into the trash can beside my desk.

Just no.

## Chapter Five

### Soren

"… TAKE THAT LEFT AT THE DUNGEON DOOR. YEAH, I know American Donkey; I was just wondering if, like, anyone else out there is as into Omar Apollo as I am. Oh hey, welcome to the stream Wanda Mabonda Eight Eleven!" I paused, following an elven NPC down a dark corridor, to read over the comments flowing in as I played *Knights of the Green Helm*. Courtney had to babysit her little sister, so she couldn't play along tonight. Which was kind of a bummer as we worked really well together. "Shit! Oh man, that rat scared me. Damn jump scares in fantasy games. Totally unexpected. Like in horror, sure, but when I'm down here in the dank with this sexy elf who has yet to reveal his real name. Cool, cool, thanks for the lurk Pistol Podunk. Yeah man, I will for sure keep rocking it to Omar. He is the man." Another comment flows in, from another follower, then another, and pretty soon, I'm talking to about ten of my fave followers and five of my subscribers. "In case you all missed the question of the day, I'll repost as soon as I get out of this dungeon, but it was asking what your fave topping on a hot dog is."

A new follower chimes, and I study the name for like a second before welcoming her to the stream.

"Hi there Granny Piano, welcome to the stream. As you can see, we're playing *Knights of the Green Helm* at the moment, working our way through a dungeon with this suspicious, but hot elf dude. Glad you could join us! Are you a Helm fan too?"

I leaned back in my chair, took a quick drink of my Sprite, and I'd blasted through homework— totally ignoring that magazine assignment because thinking of having to deal with Felix in any capacity was too depressing—and decided to stream alone for a few hours before bed. Things were going well. I had about thirty viewers, several on chat, and a new sub, Granny Piano, who typed a comment.

*Hello honey! Why are you playing such a violent game? I saw you kill a man, back there, who didn't even have arms to defend himself. Did you think about, maybe, playing that farm game that Milo likes?*

Oh. My. God. Granny Piano is my grandmother. And she just used my brother's name. Lemon-lime soda nearly spews out of my nose. I cough and try to figure out how to handle this, so I don't upset Grandma Rowe.

"Granny Piano, hello! Yeah, I did play that farm game. How are you tonight?" My brain is totally locked down. I love Grandma Rowe. She makes the best cookies in the world. And rubs my head and calls me Pumpkin. I wait in terror for her next comment to appear.

*I'm good, Pumpkin. Too much bloodshed isn't good for a young male mind, all the experts say so. Your grandfather says howdy doo and wants me to tell you that he's excited to come watch you play hockey, not this video game stuff. He's not cool like me.*

"Yeah, awesome! I can't wait to see you too."

*Are you practicing on the piano? I know, I know, but it's important to have skills other than hockey and cleaving video game bad guys in half, ask your fathers.*

"Okay, I promise I'll practice." All the other followers have gone silent. Probably, they're all sitting at home rolling on the floor at this exchange. "Oh hey, thanks for the gift sub Granny Piano! Mary Duckworth Eighty-Eight, you can now open all my cool emotes!"

*Good. So, Grandpa has some arthritis in his shoulder that's been acting up of late. We're thinking of redoing the patio next year. Screening it so Binks can go outside. That cat just loves sitting in the windows and watching the birds, so we thought we would screen in the patio and call it a catio. Grandpa came up with that. Catio. I think it's adorable, don't you?*

Yep, that was cute. My grandparents were cute as hell. Thankfully, she had to log out to go watch *Perry Mason* with my grandfather after that little bit. I think she was not into the undead cleaving either. The chat picked up after she signed out, all my subs and followers saying that they loved my granny a lot. Yeah, I did too, but I did have to have a talk with my dad about her. So, after the stream ended, I padded down the hall, past Lottie's room, where I peeked in to check on her, then past Milo's where I stuck my head in to make sure he was sleeping soundly. Sometimes, he had nightmares. Sure, I knew it wasn't only on me to protect him anymore, but old habits died really hard.

I found the younger parental unit in the TV room, splayed out over the sectional, watching a *John Wick* movie. Ten's gaze flipped from the huge set on the wall over the fireplace to me as I ambled in and sat beside him, shoving my hand into the big bowl of cheese popcorn on his lap.

"Hey," he said, then chuckled as I tried to talk and chew. Kernels of orange popcorn falling from my mouth. "Chew, then speak."

I did just that, reaching out to swipe his soda from the coffee table. "Seriously?" He asked as I chugged half the bottle down, then belched. I offered the half-empty bottle back to him, but he declined. "Keep it. I don't know where your lips have been."

"Just on my face, sadly," I sighed dramatically as Ten chuckled. "So, uhm, I got a new subscriber tonight."

I sat back and tucked my legs under my backside as John Wick went on a rampage. Good thing Grandma didn't see this movie. She thought me axing an undead dwarf was too violent.

"That's good. You're getting quite a nice fan base," he replied, his eyes on Keanu as Wick used a pencil as a deadly weapon.

"I know, I'm enjoying it a lot." He nodded as parents do when they're balancing the kid talking to them and one of their fave actors. "The new sub was Grandma."

That pulled his hazel eyes from Keanu. "Oh, that's cool. I told her about you being on Twitch, and she hurried to download it to her phone so she could follow you."

"Aww, yeah, she's the best." I nodded and bobbed my head.

Dad stared at me. "What did she do?" he asked, picking up the remote to pause the movie.

"Nothing huge. Well, she did use Milo's name in the comments." Ten grimaced. This was why I had come to him instead of Jared. Jared was cool, but older, and totally not into Twitch at all. Ten liked streaming, and he knew internet protocol, whereas Jared was not quite as up on things as Ten was. Jared was in that awkward place between Grandma and Ten. "Can you like mention to her that Twitch isn't Facebook messenger? She can't use real names or talk about personal things like Grandpa's shoulder or his gout or her choral group."

"Right, okay, yeah; I'll walk her through the basics. But go easy on her. She's just trying to be supportive of you and your hobbies. She has no clue, seriously."

"No, I know, and I love her, but she can't be so personal, that's all. I'm happy to hear about her rutabagas on messenger," I hurried to explain.

"Don't worry, I'll talk to her about it."

Jared came into the room then, fresh from a shower, his blond/silver hair still damp. He was wearing Railers fleece pants and a tee exactly like Tennant. Funny how married people started to dress alike. Funny like cringe.

"Talk to who about what?" Jared asked, lowering himself to the couch on the other side of Tennant.

"My Mom and Twitch," Ten replied as Jared looped his arm around Ten's shoulder. It was cute how affectionate they were at home. Always touching in some way. That was the kind of relationship I wanted when I finally found someone special.

"Ah, well, I'm sure things will work out. Were you playing your game online tonight?" Jared asked, Gordie padding into the room, his black nose working the air and leading him to the popcorn fest taking place. I tossed him a kernel, which he snapped out of the air.

"Yeah, and Grandma visited." I threw the dog another, then tossed one into my mouth.

"That's nice. I'm assuming you had all your homework done before you fired up the gaming computer?" Jared asked as his fingers lingered along Ten's neck, right on that cool tattoo of a roaring red lion.

"Yep, well, all that I could do alone," I replied, then sighed, the memory of having to work with Felix flaring to life like heartburn.

"Care to explain?" Jared asked, and so I did. I gave them the abridged version of things in AP English, then ate more popcorn while they exchanged glances. They knew Felix, and his family now, but only from being fellow Coyote parents. Well, not that Felix's folks showed up much to our hockey games as a couple. I think I'd seen his mom a couple of times; a cloud of perfume and teased hair was all I recalled. His dad had been more than once, but sat mostly on his phone, doing whatever stuff he thought was more important than his son. Mine did their best, but being on the road for just about the entire school year, as well as JV hockey season, they missed a lot, too. "So, we have come up with literally nothing. And really, the topic is terrible. The history of Chesterford Academy? Like, honestly, how boring? I made up some bullshit about a ghost in a closet. Honestly, if there were a ghost that would at least be something exciting."

"So, wait. He wants to do a magazine about hedge funds?" Jared enquired as Gordie drooled on the floor while he waited for more food. Me and the dog were bottomless pits according to my fathers. I could not deny. That was factual. "That's not really interesting at all, is it?"

Jared looked at Ten, who shrugged. "Not to me. If it were my project, I'd do hockey."

"See, yeah," I pointed a cheesy finger at Ten. "That's what I wanted to do, but Mr. Russell the Second was all pouty and sad, and made me feel like a loser for suggesting something so easy. He says there is some interesting history about Chesterford."

"Well, maybe he's right. Have you boys dug into ye olden days of the school and grounds? It's been sitting there for well over two hundred years. There has to be something of interest to fill up your magazine," Jared stated.

"Yeah, I guess. I don't know. This whole assignment is going to be the shits. Sorry, but this really sucks. Felix is such a snob."

"Well, maybe you just don't understand the young man. Why don't you invite him over for a study date?" Jared said and got a glance from Ten. "What? Don't kids study together anymore in person?"

"Sure we do, but I'm not sure I want that dude in my house. You've met him. He's a jerk," I argued, but Jared now seemed set on this idea.

"That's a bit extreme," Dad said with a frown. "I've seen him interacting with some of the younger students, and he seems genuinely kind to them." I rolled my eyes. "Perhaps, he's just a troubled young man living through some trying times. Surely, you can understand how hard it is to be outgoing and kind when you're caught up in a turbulent home life, and you only have to see his parents to know it's not a happy home."

I blinked at Jared. Ten nodded. Even the dog was looking at me like I was the asshole.

My sigh was legendary. Damn, but it sucked when they were right. "Okay, fine, I'll invite him over for dinner and to study."

"Good, it's a date. It's always best to be as kind as we can possibly be, even to people who annoy us at times."

"No, please, no. It is *not* a date. Not. A. Date." I stared at both of them, then at the dog, in case Gordie decided to use that D word when speaking of the possible mutual study/dinner situation. Date was a loaded word.

"I promise we will not use any words that start with D," Ten said. Jared crossed his chest. Gordie burped a sour dog belch.

"I'll ask him tomorrow in English class, but don't expect him to say yes. He's a certified dick."

I left them to their movie before they could call me out for language. Gordie followed me upstairs, taking his spot at the top of the stairs to protect us kids while we slept. I rubbed his head for a moment, gave the gremlins one final check, then crawled into bed. I browsed the web and forwarded a meme to Courtney before plugging in my phone as one of my playlists played. Lizzo and Cardi B. rapped about rumors. Not that I had to worry about talk. Felix would never agree to come to my house. He hated me too damn much.

## Chapter Six

### Felix

I COULD HEAR THE SHOUTING, EVEN OVER THE NOISE of my obnoxiously loud alarm clock, and when I switched it off, it became clear that, for some reason, Mom was visiting unannounced from New York, and she wasn't happy.

And Dad wasn't happy.

I didn't often hear Dad raise his voice to her—he was better at rolling with the verbal punches—but right now, he was shouting with intent. I knew for a fact that his new girlfriend, Cora, and idiot Tyler hadn't stayed over again because I'd told Dad, in no uncertain terms, that I didn't want them to, but whatever Mom was doing was just as bad as her finding out Dad had gotten himself a new… whatever Cora was.

Why was Mom even here? I kind of liked that she was in New York. It was quieter without her screeching all over the place.

"Yet another happy start in the Maxwell-Sinclair household," I muttered and took a shower, hoping that, maybe, all would be quiet when I was done, but no, they were still shouting. Or at least Mom was, which was par for the course. We'd, clearly, reached the familiar point in their arguments where Dad gave up and went deadly silent, and where Mom ramped up her summaries of what a shit man my dad was.

I brushed my teeth—Mom was still shouting when I finished, her shrill condemnation of something that sounded financial, drifting up the stairs and stabbing my eardrums.

I packed my school bag. Yep, still shouting.

I headed down the back stairs—anything to avoid the yelling, but the door out was locked, and I knew the damn key was in the kitchen. I contemplated climbing out of a window, but slipped past the kitchen door and hoped for the best, only Mom spotted me in the hall.

"See what you've done, Jim! My own baby won't even say hello to me! What did you say to him?" she shrieked, and her voice poked at my last nerve. Hearing my mom fight and overwhelm my dad was one thing, but being used as an emotional ball she could throw at my dad, was another. Not that my dad reacted much, he went quiet when Mom descended to using me as an example of how he had messed me up.

"I've done nothing, Terri, and maybe, that's the problem." My dad sounded tired, as if he was done with everything.

When Mom pulled me into an exaggerated hug, and I got a lung full of scent, I quickly disentangled myself from perfume and itchy fabric, and headed straight for the keys, contemplating grabbing breakfast, then deciding I was best off leaving.

"He's too skinny! Look at him!"

"No—"

"Felix, sweetheart, are you even eating?" I was so close to escaping only a few steps from the door. "Felix come back here!"

I sent up a quick prayer to the god of children living with divorcing parents and turned to face her.

"I'm going to be late for school, Mom," I managed, but that wasn't enough to stop her.

"I asked you if you are eating? Is there even food in the house?"

"Of course, I'm eating, Mom, I—"

"I won't have it, Jim, I won't let you do this to our son," she snapped, and Dad shook his head as Mom rooted about in her Gucci purse and pulled out a bundle of notes, not caring how much was there, and thrusting it at me. "Get yourself something nice," she insisted, and I didn't argue, pocketed the money, and shrugged when Dad sent me a hurt glance. Phoebe had been grocery shopping yesterday, and the refrigerator was likely close to bursting open; plus, we'd have cupboards of good stuff to eat, but me taking any money only reinforced Mom's belief that I needed cash to buy food—more ammunition in her war.

What did Dad care? The only people I was hurting here were the mom and dad who were supposed to be keeping me safe, and freaking nurturing me.

What did he want me to do? It seemed as if she'd given me over a hundred dollars, and I could add it to my savings for when I managed to get away from this family and out on my own. My college fund was in place courtesy of a grandpa I'd never met, and Mom's family was freaking loaded, but I wasn't coming back, during or after, so I'd take any cash I could get to buy my freedom. What, with the emergency hundred dad left me, I was having a good week.

*Three years until college, and then, I'm done with this shit.*

"Pack your bags, Felix," Mom snapped. "You're coming with me."

"No, Terri, he's not," Dad actually rose, almost as if he had a backbone and was going to stand between us. She sent him a look, and he slumped back into the chair and rubbed his chest, totally browbeaten.

"I said, he's coming to live with me," she snapped.

Not this again. "I'm not moving to New York, Mom," I responded with the first line of a script I knew by heart.

And her line was… "You know, you'd have your very own apartment below mine—"

Then my line went like this… "No, Mom. I go to school here. I'm staying here."

If she was that desperate to have me in her life, then she should stay here where I was vaguely happy. However, staying was an option that never occurred to her because she was with her people, and she wanted back in the fold of the Sinclair family more than she wanted to be my mom. I wasn't stupid, and after the first few times we'd had this debate, I knew taking me was more about hurting my dad, than wanting me. Not that I cared about how Dad felt when he so easily backed down—like he didn't care where I was, or what I was doing.

*I don't care who wants me or not; I'm so over all of it.*

"See what you've done?" Mom pointed at Dad.

He stared right back at her with his usual blank expression, and yet again, said absolutely nothing at all in his defense. It wasn't as if he cared where I was, and he probably already had his exit strategy with Cora and her freaking son, Tyler. Why would he need me when he could buy in a family and replace me?

Fuck it. I was done.

I headed out of the door, slamming it behind me and stepping into our beautifully manicured front yard, then headed over to the garage where Rick would be waiting to drop me at school. Instead of Rick, I saw his wife Phoebe, her of the grocery-buying, and I knew she was hiding out *here* from what was going on in *there*.

"You okay?" she asked as I sat next to her on the low wall behind the garage.

"It's all good," I lied.

"Is she taking you with her?" Phoebe sounded fearful. Of course, she did, because if I left, Dad might move, and then, he wouldn't need live-in support. No wonder she sounded so worried, when she was just another person who didn't really care about me.

Jeez, this was one hell of a pity party for one. I'm Felix Maxwell-Sinclair, and I do not wallow in shit—I pull up my big boy pants, and I make things happen.

"Stop fussing, babe," Rick said as he clapped my shoulder. "The kid's good."

I shuffled from his touch—and glanced up at him. "School?" I asked, and he nodded, because that was the most I talked to him, because who wanted to talk to a nearly sixteen-year-old kid about anything at all.

*Enough! Get my game face on.*

I hopped down from the wall, and winced when Phoebe touched my arm. "You know where we are," she murmured.

"Yep, in your tiny place over the garage," I snarked, and her eyes brightened with emotion, and I felt smaller than the smallest possible thing.

"Felix!" Rick warned.

I was digging this hole so deep, and he was frowning, and I couldn't bear any incoming lecture about being a little shit. I didn't want Rick lecturing, or Phoebe faking support, or my dad sitting silent and gray, or my mom losing her mind over some imagined issue. I was done with everyone, and it was only, what, maybe Tuesday? Wednesday?

I headed up the drive, away from the garage.

"Where are you going?" Rick called.

"I'm walking," I called back.

"It's twenty miles."

"I'll jog!"

To underscore that, I broke into a gentle jog and passed through the impressive gates and out onto the road. But I didn't carry on, turning left and heading into the hedge that masked security fencing from anyone looking. My chest was tight. I couldn't breathe, and I bent at the waist, my backpack slipping and hitting me on the back of my head so hard that I shrugged it off and let it drop to the ground, going to a crouch and wondering if this was the place I was going to die. It hurt to breathe, bands of pain circled my head, and my face was wet.

Why was my face wet? I scrubbed my hands over my skin, and peered at them, part of me expecting blood, because that would be perfect. Only it wasn't blood, so it must be freaking tears, and I don't cry.

If I started to cry, then everything would crumble.

I counted back from ten, went through the breathing exercises my obscenely expensive therapist had given me, and when I could stand without vomiting, or falling over, I picked up my pack and slipped it onto my back. Okay. Now what?

Walking to school. Being late, but at least I'd be there where I had all the control.

"Okay then," I told the hedge, and stepped back onto the sidewalk. I'd gotten a few steps when a car slowed next me. I kept walking, the car followed me, and I tilted my chin and pasted a confident expression over the angsty shit I had going on.

"Get in the car, Felix," Rick ordered, but I ignored him, because if I got in that car, all he'd do was lecture me about what I'd done, and how I'd been rude to Phoebe and how it wasn't right and… "In the car," he said, as he bumped up on the perfectly cut grass of the sidewalk and blocked my path.

I met his steady gaze, and wanted so badly to tell him that I didn't need him, but he was smiling in that kind way he had about him, and I didn't want to be late for first period English.

I liked English. That was the only reason I got into the car, but we didn't move off immediately.

"I need you to be better," he murmured, and I curled in on myself. "Please don't disrespect Phoebe. She cares for you."

*We pay you! You owe us! You're nothing!*

The hurtful words—my mom's words—spun in my head, and my headache worsened in a second, but through all of it, Rick stared at me with encouragement, and finally, I nodded. At least, he said he needed me to be better, and not that he expected me to be better. What was I doing?

"I'm sorry," I blurted.

He nodded and smiled at me. "Why don't you message her? She's fretting about you."

"She is?"

"Of course, she is, Felix. She hates to see you upset."

"I'm not upset."

He shot me a disbelieving glance, an eyebrow rising to underscore that disbelief. "Go on and message her."

I wasn't upset. What my parents did, the things I'd seen and heard, meant nothing to me, but still, I did what Rick said; sent a short message to say sorry.

Phoebe sent back fourteen hearts. I know because I counted each of them, and somehow, those tiny hearts created a cap over the hole inside me, so much that, by the time I got to school, I had my mask back in place.

---

MR. RUSSELL WAS AN ASSHOLE. THERE WAS NO other word for it when, the moment the class started, he was asking about the projects. Soren had wanted to talk about it before homeroom, but I ignored him. He demanded that we at least think about it before class. I ignored him, then, as well, turning my back on him because I really couldn't deal with the condemnation in his dark eyes. And now, the minute we sat down, Mr. Russell wanted to see what we'd come up with so far, and was busy walking around and chatting to people, and thank god, we were at the back of the room.

"Did you do it?" Soren asked.

I rolled my eyes at him. "No."

"But you took the paper," he faux-whispered.

"*But you took the paper*," I repeated and faked a whine, which sounded nothing like Soren, but made me feel better.

His lips thinned. "Pathetic," he muttered and opened his pad to tear off a sheet. He hurriedly titled it the same as yesterday and drew four boxes under it, glancing at me, and shaking his head. Then, he stared at the empty sheet, and through all of this, Mr. Russell was moving toward us.

"Foundation, Alumni," I muttered, and after a pause, when I expected him to laugh in my face, he added the two titles, then tapped his pen on the paper.

Mr. Russell was at the desks in the row in front of

us, and when I glanced over, I could see copious notes, and I quickly reached over and snatched the paper from Soren. He went to grab it, but I was too fast—take that Soren I'm-fast-on-ice Madsen-Rowe —and I scrawled two more headings and, then, random words under each of them.

"Felix? Soren? What have you come up with? I'm so excited to see where you take this project."

Soren sent me a look, one that said we were fucked, but I cleared my throat. "We're looking at the history of the school, but not just of the school itself, but of the people - the founders, the alumni—how war affected the people who went here and the teachers, how world events shaped the curriculum. It will be an extensive project based on people."

"People," Mr. Russell said wonderingly.

"People shape history, Mr. Russell," I said, and got an enthusiastic nod.

"That is so good. Keep it up."

As soon as Mr. Russell moved back to the front of the class to start the lesson proper, I turned to Soren and shoved the paper on the desk. I gave him the best and smuggest smile I had going, and assumed he'd have something to snark back at me. Instead, he nodded, then offered a fist.

"Nice one," he murmured, and waited for me to bump his fist, which I didn't do because… Soren.

Still, I felt like today had at least one achievement on the good side of the list, and Soren's praise sparked a tiny something in my chest, and I think it was something like pride.

Go figure.

## Chapter Seven

### Soren

COOL. FELIX HAD SAVED OUR ASSES WITH HIS QUICK thinking.

I'd never thought the dude was dumb, obviously he wasn't, or he wouldn't be at Chesterford, despite his daddy's dineros. Man, I needed to stop watching old gangster movies late at night. But yeah, Felix was smart, but a jerk. A smart jerk. I shot him a look out of the corner of my eye, and there was a cuteness to him when he wasn't sneering or being the King of the Jerks. I'd just moved him up the royal ladder from prince to king; although, maybe his father was the king. Okay, yeah, Prince of Jerks. Him and Joffrey Baratheon.

"So," I said after several minutes of utter silence from my project partner dragged by. He huffed, blue eyes narrowed. "We'll need to flesh all this out."

He stared blankly at me, then straightened his tie. I glanced down to see mine had oatmeal on it. Shit. I rubbed at the glob with the eraser of my pencil.

"That won't erase food you moron," Felix snarked. I rubbed harder. He huffed. "You'll have to wash it out in the sink between classes."

"Yeah." I sighed and dropped my tie. Jared's voice popped into my head. Look for the good in people, he was known to say. I stared at Felix. He pretended not to see me gawking at him as Mr. Russell blathered on about some guy named Moss who was editor-in-chief of *New York* magazine. "Your tie is nice. Clean." He glanced my way with a raised eyebrow. "No food on it."

"I wasn't raised in a sty," he fired back. Ouch. Right. I counted to ten, then nudged him in the side so hard he nearly tumbled out of his seat. Mr. Russell looked our way, smiled, and then, went back to talking about editing magazines and how much of an impact magazines had and blah, blah, blah. Cue Charlie Brown teacher voice.

"Good one. So, yeah, fleshing out. Why don't you come to my house tonight, and we can work." I tapped the paper with four boxes and nothing else. Man, we had a long way to go on this.

He sat there dumbfounded. "Come to your house?"

"Yeah, to study. Well, not only study. Just to research on some of this crap. My grandparents might be there as well, but maybe not until tomorrow. They moved up here from down south this summer so they could help babysit when my dads have to travel. Also, because it's closer to most of the grandkids, aside from Ryker, who's in Arizona, and my uncle Jamie, who's down in Florida. So, yeah, it might be us and the parental units and grandparents. Maybe, depends on if Grandma and Grandpa are doing their ballroom dancing classes tonight. They might be…"

"I don't need a rundown of your stupid family calendar. I can't come."

"Oh, sure, I kind of figured that. Do you want me to come to your place?"

"No!"

I drew back at the snap of his words. "Okay," I held up my hands in mock surrender.

"No, I forgot that I *don't* have a date tonight." A date? Who was he dating? Cruella De Vil? Captain Hook? No, not Hook. Dude wasn't queer, or if he was, he was hiding that shit deep. Like center of the earth, *Land of the Lost* deep. "I can come over."

"Oh-kay. Good. So do you know anything about the people who went here in the olden days?"

"Like the seventies?"

"Sure, maybe, or even older. Like during the wars. We could talk to Desmond, the janitor. He's old and has been around here forever."

Felix frowned. "'The janitor'?" Then, he stared at me as if I had a penguin doing long division on my head.

"Yeah, Desmond, old guy, pushes around a mop and yells at people to pick up their damn trash."

The look he gave me would have melted a lesser man. "I know what a fucking janitor does, Rowe. Fine, we'll talk to him sometime, but I can't think what a man who cleans up after assholes like us would have to tell us that would be slightly entertaining."

I shrugged. The bell rang. Felix was up and out of his seat in a flash. I grabbed my backpack from the floor and raced to catch up to him in the hall. I sidestepped the basketball team as they moved by in a pack. Christen, the team captain, gave me a fist to tap as I jogged past.

"Hey, Sinclair," I called, smiling sweetly at

Chelsea, who gave me a demure finger wave from amid a group of ten girls. They all giggled and whispered as I raced past. Felix was chugging along with due intent. "Hey, you need my address," I said as I caught up to him outside the English department staff lounge. He swung around, glowering, and brushed my hand from his shoulder. I raised my hands, palms out. "Dude, relax."

"Do *not* touch me, Rowe."

"If you, maybe, stopped when I called, I wouldn't have had to touch your royalness."

"Fuck all the way off."

The urge to punch that elite button nose was strong. "Dude, just let me give you my address, or do you plan to have your chauffeur drive you all over Harrisburg seeking out my place?"

He stared at me as if willing himself to develop laser eye beams à la Homelander. When that didn't happen, he pulled his phone out of his pocket, tapped in his security code, then passed it to me. I entered my info, then held out the slim black cell as the halls began to empty.

"Are you taking this or what? I have to get to AP Chinese." I shoved it at him.

He slowly plucked it from my hand, then gave it a cursory glance. "I'll be there at six."

He spun and sped off. I studied him as he went, wondering what it was about the guy that could make me feel extreme ire at him one second, then some sort of unrecognizable sadness the next. The warning bell rang.

"Shit!" I took off at Mach and skidded into class just as the second, and final, bell rang.

Ms. Chen glanced at her watch, then at me. "Cutting it close, aren't we, Mr. Madsen-Rowe?"

I nodded, slunk to my seat, and gave Courtney a wink. Close did not only count in horseshoes and hand grenades, as Grandpa said. It also counted in getting to class on time.

———

GUESS FELIX HAD ONE THING GOING FOR HIM. Punctuality.

He rang our doorbell at exactly six p.m. on the dot.

Who the hell shows up precisely on time? It was bizarre. *He* was bizarre.

Still, I let him in, catching a dark sedan waiting out on the street. Felix stood on the stoop in jeans, a tank top with the evil Stay-Puft Marshmallow man on it, and top-of-the-line Nikes. His hair was combed, his gaze darting around behind me like he feared he might be walking into a *Silent Hill* home or something. I glanced back to see the dog bounding toward us, tongue out, Lottie running after the Lab with a magic wand and one bare foot. She tended to lose socks and shoes. Ten called it her special gift.

"Brace yourself," I told Felix. He spread his feet, eyes wide, as Gordie hit him at full speed. I lunged for his collar as Lottie shouted out magic spells to make the dog sit and be good. Her magic needed work. Gordie greeted Felix as he did everyone: tail wagging, tongue washing, back paws tapping in glee. "Sit, sit, sit, sit."

"Sit damn it!" Lottie shouted as she fired another imaginary spell at the bouncing chocolate Lab/drool monster. I snorted at her cussing. That was Ten, totally. If he said that once during the day, he said it a thousand times. "Hello, pretty boy. Welcome to our house. This is Gordie, who is not good from puppy training school."

Lottie held out her hand for a shake, while I struggled to get the dog out of Felix's shocked face. To his credit, he didn't lose his shit. Probably, because Lottie was there smiling up at him with her little sticky hand extended.

"Four-foot rule," I grunted to the pooch as I

steered his front legs toward the floor. "All four feet stay on the floor, remember?" I asked and got a short happy woof.

"He does not remember at all. Excuse me, pretty boy, I am waiting." She shook her hand at Felix, who appeared to be a bit out of things. His cheeks were flushed and coated with dog spit, his tidy hair was sticking up, and his eyes were round. Lottie was right. He *was* a pretty boy. "My name is Charlotte Madsen-Rowe."

"Oh, uhm Felix." He seemed to gather himself and bent down to shake her hand. Gordie, who was now sitting, but just, woofed again. "It's a pleasure to meet you, Miss Charlotte."

She curtsied, then ran off, the dog dashing after her. Milo came thundering down the stairs, then paused to stare at Felix openly.

"Was that your guest?" Jared called, following my brother from upstairs. "Oh, yes, it is. Come in, Felix. We were just washing up before dinner. I hope you like spaghetti. It's the one dish that Tennant can prepare that won't set off the smoke alarms."

"I heard that!" Ten shouted from the kitchen.

Felix stood just inside the door now, gaping at Jared as my dad herded Milo into the kitchen. You had to get him to the table fast after a hand wash, or he would end up dirty in the blink of an eye. That was Milo's special gift.

"You can wash the dog spit off here," I said, easing him into the madness, then closing the front door. I led him to a small washroom off the living room. It was peach and white with a toilet and sink, but no shower. "Do you want me to wait outside to guide you to the kitchen?"

"Please." He closed the door with a snap right in my face.

I drew in a long breath, let it out through my nose, and told myself to find a moment of Zen. I made my way to the kitchen. Ten was at the stove stirring pasta. Jared was buckling Lottie into a booster seat, and Milo was feeding Gordie a garlic breadstick. Ten looked at me over his shoulder.

"Where's your friend?" he asked, lifting a strand out of the water, then blowing on it. He liked it firm, while Jared preferred it well done. The pasta doneness battle happened weekly around here.

"Please cook that a little longer," Jared said as he padded to the fridge for drinks.

"Yep." Ten turned off the heat with a wink at me.

"He's not really my friend. He's a teammate and project co-worker," I clarified as I pulled out my seat.

"Go wait for him. It's not polite to let him wander

around looking for us," Jared stated as he pulled a gallon of milk from the fridge.

I huffed, then walked back up the hall to wait like a jackass for Felix. When he stepped out, hair wet and stuck to his head, and his face pink from scrubbing, he gave me a glower.

"Do not even," I said with attitude. "Dad made me come back. This way." I led him back to the kitchen. "Here he is. All safe and sound. Good thing I was there to guide him here, or he may have wandered into the toy room where he would never be heard from again."

Jared and Ten both shot me those I'm-amused-but-I'm-pretending-to-not-be expressions. "Welcome to our home, Felix," Jared said with a smile, then poured some milk into Milo's glass. "I'm Jared, and that's Ten over there undercooking the spaghetti."

Ten waved a spaghetti fork in the air in greeting. "Nice to meet you, Felix."

"It's a real honor to be here," Felix said, standing at an empty chair stiff as a stick.

"Dude, this isn't military school, you can sit and chill," I whispered, giving Felix a nudge that snapped the look of adoration he was wearing. That was common when people met Jared and Ten, mostly Ten. Especially, if the person getting the meet-and-greet was a hockey player or had any knowledge of sports at all. Ten was a generational phenomenon, a future Hockey Hall of Fame inductee, and one of the biggest stars in hockey. I'd been kind of starstruck at first, too, but now he was just Dad.

Felix blushed, then dropped into his seat, his backpack resting on his lap. Jared chuckled, then lifted the pack from his legs and draped it over the back of his chair. Ten carried a huge bowl of spaghetti and meatballs—Grandma made them and froze them —to the table. Jared brought a bowl of greens to the table, the salad topped with tiny tomatoes, carrot slivers, and cucumber wedges.

"Dig in," Ten said as he sat next to Lottie.

We started filling plates with steaming pasta, the aroma of tomato sauce and garlic filling the wide and homey kitchen. Felix looked so out of place here. His shoulders were firm, his jaw tight, and his lips flat.

"So, Felix, are you looking forward to the new Coyotes season?" Jared asked, sprinkling some bacon bits on his salad, then passing the bottle to Ten.

Lottie plucked a piece of cucumber from her salad and shoved it into her mouth. She would only eat the cukes. Milo was picking off the carrot shavings.

"Yes, sir, very much," Felix replied, his plate and salad bowl still empty.

"Good, I was just talking to Ten about your team this year. I know you lost a few key players when the juniors and seniors went to varsity, but your defensive core is strong. I think that, with some intense training, they can easily make up for the loss of Johnson and Waite."

Ten joined in. "Totally. The forwards are in good shape. I'd be happy to stop by someday during practice and spend time on the ice with you guys," he said as he twirled some spaghetti onto his fork.

Gordie whimpered under the table, softly, only to remind us he was there and starving. Not really. He had been fed ten minutes ago so he wouldn't put on the woe-is-me-I-is-so-hangry show when we had company.

"Really?" Felix asked breathlessly. Ten smiled and nodded. "That would be incredible. Really incredible. Really good, I mean, that would be really good."

And then, he smiled. Felix Maxwell-Sinclair smiled an honest-to-goodness smile that reached his eyes, and he was transformed. My forkful of spun spaghetti sat right on my bottom lip as I stared in wonder at the transformation a smile could make to a guy. Yeah, Lottie was more than right.

Felix wasn't just pretty, he was gorgeous.

## Chapter Eight

### Felix

I CHECKED THE PAGE TACKED TO THE WALL FOR OUR first practice that was actually on the ice. This wasn't the final lines set in stone, this was based on Coach Sennett's knowledge of us from last year, but I still felt a small thrill that I'd retained second line status in Coach's head. Also, that he hadn't put me anywhere near stupid ass Soren, or that Tyler kid. As expected Shaun was our captain.

**First Line**

C - #3 Shaun Stanton (Captain) –
Sophomore

LW - #10 Will Bradrick – Sophomore

RW - #34 – Gavin Neely - Sophomore

## Second Line

C: #19 - Jonathan McCombs -
Freshman

LW: #14 - Jack Neeley – Freshman

RW: #17 - Felix Maxwell-Sinclair -
Sophomore

## Third Line

C: #21 - Caleb Baker - Sophomore

LW: #16 - Soren Madsen-Rowe -
Sophomore

RW: #18 - Tyler Corrigan - Sophomore

## Fourth Line

C: #15 - Carson Britt - Sophomore

LW: #46 - Auden Smith - Sophomore

RW: #56 - Asher Perez – Sophomore

## Defense 1

D: #2 - Michael Ponatello - Freshman

D: #4 - Mark Anderson - Sophomore

**Defense 2**

#6 - Riley Jackson - Freshman

#22 - Dominic Wishor - Sophomore

**Defense 3**

#24 - Lance King - Sophomore

#41 - Seth Foster - Freshman

**Goal**

G1 - #31 - Elijah Carter-Collins III –
Catches L – Freshman

G2 - #40 - Cullen Perry - Catches L -
Sophomore

"NICE," JOHNNY SAID AT MY SIDE, AND WE FIST-bumped. Mom always said it was who you knew that got you places, and Johnny's dad was in funding, and I liked to keep in with Johnny in case my link to him paved the way for a bright future. Not that we were friends—for some reason, he didn't want to be friends, at least not the kind who hung out. I didn't seem to attract friends like that, just people like Jonah and Miles who, y'know, weren't really *friends* as such.

Who needs friends anyway?

"It's not like it's the final list," Jack pointed out, our penciled-in left wing. He knew—we all knew—Jack was too good to stay on the second line forever. Just like his big brother, Gavin, out on the first line, he was destined to go professional—everyone said so. What level of professional was up for debate, but they were both obsessed with a future career on the ice. I stayed out of the petty bickering between the brothers, as I didn't really care.

"Who moved Soren up to the third line?" Auden asked, frowning at the paper, probably pissed he'd been relegated to fourth line and Soren had been slotted in his place.

"It's not for his skills on ice," I said, and left the comment dangling. Auden glanced my way and nodded. "You think…?"

"Maybe one of his new daddies paid for a place," I deadpanned, and saw Auden's eyes widen, frantically flicking from me to something behind me.

It had to be Soren—him of the perfect freaking dinner party family thing, with his cute as a button stepsister, and his idiot brother who'd stared at me the whole night. Fuck them and their niceness, and Ten promising he'd visit the rink, and Jared being all serious and asking me questions about planned vacations (what vacations, my family didn't do vacations), my future (money), and my favorite hockey team (Railers first, LA Storm second, and it's a big no to Boston, for reasons).

"Guess getting picked out of the gutter by hockey royalty works," I said, then casually turned to find Soren right behind me as I expected. I raked my gaze from his perfect flicky hair down to his scuffed shoes and back up again before tilting my chin. "Oops," I murmured, and braced myself for a punch, or a tussle, or just some pointed defensive words. He gave me a look, one that I couldn't fully decipher, but which spoke volumes about his opinion of me.

Whatever.

"Third line, Rowe," I muttered in case he hadn't seen, "with weak-ass Tyler on your wing. Jeez, I feel sorry for Caleb being stuck with you two."

"I'm happy to be there with Soren and Tyler," Caleb appeared at my side, and offered a fist to Soren, who smiled with genuine happiness at the new arrival. I used to like Caleb in a weird sort of way—after all, he played the violin, and we'd connected in music class—but fuck him. If he was happy to play with Soren, then that marked him down in my ledger of... well, my ledger of whatever.

"Me too," Tyler added.

I wondered when in hell the brat forcing his way into my family had turned up. You'd better believe I faced him down immediately, and watched as his shoulders dropped, and he moved a step closer to Soren.

"You won't be when Soren fucks up," I said, and brushed imaginary lint from Soren's jacket. To his credit, he didn't flinch, but I noticed the way his fist clenched at his side. Oh, how I'd love another visit to the principal where I got to explain how awful I felt after Soren hit me. A year back, I'd provoked him, and he'd hit me so hard that I'd bounced off a locker, fuck, did he get in trouble for that one. I didn't come out looking as shiny as I'd hoped, and it didn't work anyway, because neither of my parents bothered to turn up for the meeting, but still, it had been satisfying watching his rescuers, aka his parents, take him out of the office.

Soren and I had an epic stare-off, and then, he muttered a curse under his breath and headed for the changing rooms, with Tyler and Caleb in tow, then the rest of the team followed, and I strolled in last, as if I didn't give a shit which cubby I sat in. The only space left was by our captain Shaun Stanton, and he side-eyed me when I sat down, but he didn't tell me to move. Take that team, I'm next to the freaking captain.

We got ready to get out on the ice, waiting around for Coach to come in with his usual speech for our first time out on the ice practice, but I was itching to start playing some hockey. I'd missed it over the summer, although Mom had gotten me a ton of ice time when I'd visited her in New York, and even though it was so I wasn't in her hair, I'd enjoyed the mini-summer school and learned some good things—things I was going to dazzle the rest of the team with when our blades hit the cold stuff.

"Our game against Hershey is in five weeks. Between then and now, I want to see solid practice, and that includes time in the gym for…" I tuned out because it was the same this year as it had been the last. "…Madsen-Rowe." I snapped back to whatever he was saying and saw that everyone was whispering, and there were even a few whoops. My gaze immediately went to Soren, but he was staring at the floor, and I wondered if, maybe, he'd had a reprimand or something?

"Fuck yes! I hope he brings Stan with him," Elijah, our goalie, said from across the room.

"And Adler! I love Adler," Riley shouted back at him as the volume of noise in the room grew.

"Settle down! Settle down!" Coach shouted over the noise, then blew his whistle, which made us all stop. "As far as I'm aware, Mr. Madsen-Rowe will be attending on his own, and not, in fact, bringing the entire Harrisburg Railers team with him." Coach looked pointedly at Soren, who blushed scarlet and bent to fuss over the taping on his stick.

His Tennant Madsen-Rowe stick.

I had the same one, but I had to buy mine. I bet he got a lot of shit for free—jerseys and stuff—although, it didn't worry me what I had to pay for, given I had generational money, or rather my mom did, and all I had to do was pin her down to ask, or if I was being particularly devious, send texts to both her and my dad so they played off against each other. Not that Dad played that game anymore, in fact, Dad was becoming less of the dad I knew, and more like… I dunno. He was asking me about school, and trying to show an interest.

Fuck that noise.

Why wasn't Soren keeping his head up, proud of what he'd managed to do by getting his dad here? He'd done the impossible, and all because of who had taken him in—he had one over the rest of us. Why wasn't he freaking happy?

"...so, I'd like you all to come armed with meaningful questions for our guest, and I know I can rely on you all to pull together as a team and show him what the Coyotes are made of. Go Coyotes!"

"Go Coyotes!" we replied as a team.

But I was more interested in Soren's embarrassment, than a rallying cry, and that image of him all pink-cheeked went out on the ice with me. He'd seen me at my most vulnerable, when I got all excited about his parent coming to the school—hell, he'd seen me basically faint at the table, or near enough damn it, at the thought of being able to talk to Tennant, let alone actually get to be on the ice with him.

The poster of Ten was my biggest, and he was every fantasy I'd ever had rolled into one. Had the fantasy dimmed when I saw him get into a spaghetti fight with Milo? Nope. Was it tarnished when he and Milo went on to have a burping contest? Nope. My obsession with him didn't waver one single bit, even if it turned out that away from the rink, he was a normal person.

Not like Soren, whom I caught staring at me during that dinner with an expression of shock, or something equally shit, as if he was commenting on me getting excited. I didn't want to get laughed at. I didn't want Soren judging me, and the resentment had been seething and roiling inside me since the moment he'd packed up his pens and suggested we were done for the night. Thankfully, we'd been working in the dining room, and not in his bedroom, and I'd managed to get, yet, more sightings of Tennant and his husband.

They were affectionate to the point of nauseating, but even that didn't take the shine off my hero, and I had to admit—privately—that it was weird and unsettling to see a *normal* family doing *normal* things. Jared had even asked us about our project, sitting at the table and talking history, and had given us a link to some historical society run by a friend of a friend, who apparently would be happy for us to visit. He told us that he'd missed out on working on projects for his other son, Ryker, yet another hockey player who was out there shining and living his best life, albeit for the Arizona Raptors, a team I really didn't follow.

At least, Ryker was his son by blood, not a lucky throwaway he'd picked up like Soren and Milo; although, wisely, I kept that thought to myself.

*I'm not jealous.*

"Earth to Felix," Coach snapped his fingers in front of my face.

I stiffened. "Yes coach?"

"You're just sitting there…" He waved at me and, then, the room.

I realized everyone else had left the room, and I fiddled with my lace as if that was the delay, then rolled up and fake-saluted him. "On my way, Coach."

"Felix?"

I stopped at the edge of the corridor leading to the ice and turned back to face him. "Yes Coach?"

"Don't repeat last year. Keep it clean, because however good you are out there, if you escalate…" He raised an eyebrow and didn't have to finish because it was a warning to keep my nose clean, and it was the same thing he said to me every single time he pulled me from the herd. So what, if I tended to steamroll skaters? So what if I used the game to work out tension? All I heard in all of that was the fact that he said I was good.

I'd take that win any day.

The moment my skates hit the ice, I felt a kind of peace wash over me. This was my arena, my battleground, and the anxiety that I held in my shoulders slipped away one glide at a time. I didn't feel wobbly, or unsure, or less of a son, or lonely, or angry, or anything when I was on the ice. I had power here—over each glide, over each hit of the puck—and filled with excitement for the year, I stopped right in front of our goalie, showering him with snow.

"Asshole!" Elijah shouted, but he was grinning at me, and I couldn't help but smile in return. We were back.

## Chapter Nine

### Soren

"...ON SOME HIGH-SPEED DRILLS, WORKING ON TAKING passes on the forehand and backhand, and some one-touch passes. This will help us refresh ourselves after a long summer off, and also, show me where we may need more help with passing drills in the future," Coach was saying as we knelt on the ice around him and the two volunteer coaches. My sight kept darting to Felix, kneeling a few guys over, his shiny yellow hair peeking out from the back of his skid lid, glowing like spun gold under the bright lights of the rink. There was something different about him. I'd seen a softer side to him at dinner, just for a minute or two, and it was like someone had flipped a switch in my head. I mean, the guy was still a jerk, but now, I knew he could be decent. He'd actually smiled. Not at me, obviously, but at Ten, which showed that he *could* be nice.

Studying him closely as he stared at Coach, I couldn't help but notice his profile. Even with the full-face cage, I could enjoy the view. Felix was really good-looking, even if in repose, he held his chin up in that snooty way rich folks did. He nodded along with whatever Coach was now drawing on his beloved white board—the man must sleep with that white board, which probably made his wife mad – then wet his lips. My dick took notice, which freaked me out to the point that I choked on some spit, and everyone on the ice gaped at me gagging.

"Wrong pipe," I coughed out, working up a smile as I hacked up a lung.

Felix stared at me for a long time, then shook his head and went back to paying attention. Which was what I should be doing instead of wondering why I had never noticed the way his hair curled at the back of his neck or that he had a dimple. In my defense, I had never seen the dude smile before, so that dimple was a hidden weapon. His skin was clear, his eyes bright blue, and his cheeks covered with a fine patina of sweat. If he turned his head just right, I could see the golden whiskers above his upper lip and along his jaw. When had he started shaving? Did he shave a lot? I ran a razor over my face three times a week, but I was dark haired, and Felix was not. I bet he had delicate skin, so maybe, he only shaved once a week or—

"Please repeat what I just said, Mr. Madsen-Rowe?"

I blinked back into the moment. Everyone was waiting for me to reply. Shit.

"Uhm, well, I think, we should all work really hard on the passing aspect of our game." Then, I hit Coach with a brilliant smile. "We all should go out, play hard, and work every day on our game."

"To quote Tennant Rowe," Cullen, one of our goalies, chimed in. Oh right, *that* was where I had heard that. I thought Joe Thornton had said it. My bad.

The guys snickered. Felix rolled his eyes.

I got a hearty sigh from Coach. "Goes without saying. What I was explaining to you gentlemen was that it's important to hone our passing skills now, so that we don't have as many turnovers as we did last season. I want crisp, clean passes, tape to tape, on a steady rotation down the ice to the goalie where we will take the shot. Now, I want you to pair up for this drill. Goalies, please get settled in your nets while we set up the cones."

People paired up fast. I glanced around, and it was only me and Felix unpaired. Which yeah, I totally got. No one wanted to deal with Felix. He was *a pill* as Grandma would say, but, and this was a big but, I'd seen a softer side of him. Just a glimpse, but it was there, buried under a thousand layers of asshole. Knowing I'd probably pay for my kindness, I skated over to him and met his suspicious look with a shrug.

"Guess it's you and me," I said as the coaches set up cones at center ice, ringing the Coyotes logo, then blowing on their whistles.

"Whatever," Felix mumbled around his mouthguard. Cool. Happy times right ahead. Blowing out a breath, I dug deep for that inner nice guy who was living inside me. He'd been hidden too, for a long time, when Milo and I were bouncing from foster to foster. One of the first lessons I had learned being in the system was, if you let people in, you got hurt. Even now, I tended to keep the big things close to my chest, but living with Ten and Jared was changing that. I was willing to open up, a little, with my dads and grandparents. And that trust leached into other people. Felix, I suspected, was hiding his inner tenderness for some reason. Knowing how that road felt under a man's shoes, I figured I could, maybe, stroll it along with him. Or maybe, he would tell me to leave him the hell alone. Totally his right.

"Cool. You go first. I'll hang back and take the pass from you." I reached out to tap the top of his helmet.

He stared at me as if I'd lost my mind. "Don't touch me," he replied icily, then spun to face Coach. Yeah, it was going to be one long-ass road. Long. Ass. Road. Like to Australia from Pennsylvania long. "And don't mess shit up with your lousy puck-handling skills," he flung back over his shoulder.

Man, he was making it hard to be nice. "You just worry about *your* lousy puck-handling skills."

There. Showed him.

Not.

Felix peeled out, picked up the puck Coach passed to him, then turned to face the goalie at the home end of the ice. I broke away from the boards to retrieve his pass, then fired it back to him as we cruised down the ice. He didn't have bad puck-handling skills at all. He wasn't Patrick Kane, but then again, I wasn't Sidney Crosby or Tennant Rowe. If only I could inhale Ten's talents on the air. Like a cold, just mad puck skills.

We rolled up at the goalie, and I put a mediocre

pass right on his tape. The tendie moved with the pass to block the shot with ease. I gave Elijah a thumbs up to bolster his confidence. His nerves were obvious still, even though he'd made the cut.

"Not too bad," Felix said as we glided to the back of the line to wait for our turn.

"Thanks. If the puck hadn't been on its side and so wobbly, you'd have had a better shot opportunity," I replied as I leaned over the boards to find a water bottle.

He stared at me openly, blue eyes wide behind his grill. "Yeah, well, do better," he replied, but the comeback lacked any real fire.

The other guys in front of us kept peeking back over their well-padded shoulders, confusion on their faces. Guess they were trying to figure out why I was being so nice to such a dick. I was kind of wondering that myself. I mean, sure it was the nice thing to do, and my dads were all about doing the kind and right thing. And yeah, he was pretty fit. Totally DDG to be honest. But him being drop-dead gorgeous had little to do with… Nah, it had a lot to do with it. Hashtag shallow Soren.

We spent an hour on passing drills, and when Coach dismissed us, we were all more than ready. Showers were first. Obvs. I could smell myself when we'd come off the ice. Talk and laughter filled the locker room, then flowed into the massive shower room. Several of us made plans to head to Hot Pot Noodle Shop afterwards for some killer ramen. Without a doubt, *the* best ramen in Pennsylvania, no lie.

Exiting the shower, towel around my waist, funky Railers crocs squeaking on my wet feet, I spied Felix wiggling into a pair of jeans. His back was to me, still damp, and I couldn't turn away. The dude was sleek, but firm, nice shoulders narrowing to a lean waist, and that bubble butt that all hockey players had to deal with. A really nice view if I did say so myself. Something under my towel twitched. Felix turned then, his eyes narrowing, catching me ogling his ass. Heat spread up my chest to my face.

*Quick, Soren, think of something to say!*

"So, some of the guys are going to Hot Pot Noodle for some ramen and team bonding. You want to go?" I blurted out, feeling the dark looks from the others who were part of the soup brigade. Felix gaped at me, stunned, his eyebrows beetling as he tried to triangulate my offer. "Like, if you don't want to or have a date or are buried in homework, I totally get that."

There, I gave him an out.

He flicked a look at the other guys milling around, then nodded slowly. Just once. "Sure, okay," he mumbled, then turned his back to me again.

"Cool, cool, cool," I whispered to myself, dashing to my locker with such shameful speed I lost a croc and had to hop over on one foot to get it because my teammates were dicks who would rather watch me hop, than toss me my croc. I flipped them all off.

"Hey," Shaun said as he sidled up to me. I glanced to the right as I stepped into my board shorts. "Look, I'm cool with Felix coming. I mean he needs to integrate into the team more, and you're the perfect one to guide him in." I was? Why was that? "The thing is, Tyler is coming for soup too, right, and that's going to make things really awkward." Shit. I bit down on the inside of my cheek. "I'm not saying Felix can't come, but since you and him seem to be buddies now—"

"Dude, we're not buddies. We're just…I don't know, working on this magazine project together, and we're just…stuck doing that, and I thought, he might be less of a sphincter, if he spent time with the team."

"No, hey, I totally get that, but if he starts stirring the shit pot, I will ask him to leave."

I nodded. Shaun was the JV captain for a reason. He loved this team and hockey almost more than he loved his dog, Pete. And he loved Pete. The dude took that little pug dog just about everywhere he went. Pete was our unofficial team mascot.

"That's cool. Totally. And I will back you if he breaks out his asshole personality."

Shaun clapped my shoulder, then walked off. Right. Message received. I hurried to dress, then shucked my Chesterford duffel onto my shoulder. Then, I grabbed my equipment bag, zipped it fast because there was some funk wafting out of it, and went over to the doorway to wait for Felix. Everyone else was already gone, but he was fiddling with his hair, making it look tousled and flicked and bouncy. The gold strands appeared to be super soft. Like his lips.

"Do I have something on my face, Rowe?" He barked, jolting me from the study of his mouth.

My face pinked again. "Nope, I'm just amazed. I've never seen a guy with a face that looks so much like a baboon's butt before."

He sniffed in that way that he did, and I chuckled at the big middle finger he held up right in front of my face. I swatted it aside. We walked out of the barn, not talking, but side-by-side, the warm winds blowing the scent of coconut into my face. I really liked his shower scents. Maybe, I'd ask

Grandma for a coconut cake for Sunday dinner this week.

Hot Pot Noodle Shop was down the block from the Chesterford campus. It sat on a side street facing the elementary school, tucked among a flower shop, a bookstore where we were encouraged to buy our school supplies, and several other stores in a glitchy strip mall.

The inside of the noodle shop was pure anime neon joy. Bright-colored tables, walls, and floors grabbed your attention right off, adding a frenetic vibe that meshed perfectly with the neon signs of various anime animals eating ramen. A Lizzo tune was thumping out of the speakers hidden throughout the eatery. The place was hopping, most all the tables were filled, but we found two near the kitchen and tugged them close. Felix plopped down at one end of the tables, Tyler at the other, and the rest of us filled the gaps.

Shaun sat on one side of Felix, and I took the other. Felix was sullen it seemed, uncharacteristically silent as he perused the menu.

"You ever come here before?" I asked, not even needing to know what I was getting. My usual. Kimchi, fried dumplings, and spicy chicken ramen. Oh, and a tall grape soda.

"No," Felix replied, glancing up from the menu to cast a withering glance at the busy restaurant. They did a killer business being so close to a school. Who didn't love ramen? "It's not exactly my type of place."

I tossed Shaun a questioning look. Our captain rolled his eyes, then went back to checking out the food choices.

"We come here all the time after practices," I said, trying to be cheery and upbeat.

"Yes, I know. I was never invited before," Felix replied with all the warmth of a walk-in freezer.

Oh shit, okay, well, that was brutally honest. Now, I felt bad. Why though? The guy was a stuck-up jerk to everyone who happened to wander into his firing range. Why was his being a pariah my worry?

"Well, now you're invited. So hey, if you've not been here before, I highly recommend the kimchi for starters," I gushed, hoping we could move past the social snubbing that had taken place previously. It was kind of his fault that we'd not asked him to come. He was always so cold, so mean, so outright violent at times. Plus, we all liked Tyler. Everyone did. So him always being a dick to Tyler kind of placed him on the outside looking in, right?

The server arrived and took our orders. Then, we

all leaned in to talk about life. Hockey, girls, guys, teachers, homework, sports, movies—whatever anyone thought of. We chatted about a YouTuber who was racking up viewers with her offbeat takes on movies. Then, we dished about a guy on Twitch who was recently banned. Tyler brought up a new show on Netflix about a gay teenager who was really a shapeshifter.

I glanced at Felix when that topic came up. He was too busy eating tiny fried dumplings to look pissy. He had some talent with the chopsticks. It had taken me months to learn how to eat with them. Felix had that shit down.

"…lead is played by the same guy who was in that queer show about the football player over in the UK," Tyler said around a mouthful of soft-boiled egg from his pork ramen bowl.

"David Anthony Hayes," Felix tossed out blithely, his lips smeared with pink, sweet dipping sauce from the dumplings. They seemed incredibly kissable… "He used to play soccer for real at his school before he got that part. I loved that show. Pity it only ran for three seasons."

We all fell dumb, chopsticks in hands, staring at Felix as if he had a quintet of macaws reading *Othello* atop his head.

"I didn't think you liked queer content," Tyler chanced from the far end of the table.

Felix stared at Tyler hard, his cheeks flushing as he lowered his chopsticks. "I don't know what you're talking about, but I have nothing against queer anything."

My mouth fell open an inch. Huh. Okay, well that was news. Maybe, I'd assumed Felix disliked Tyler because he was out, but that didn't seem to be the case. Curiouser and curiouser. Now that I thought harder on it—the talk at the table coming back to center on who was hooking up with whom already this year—Felix seemed to have no discomfort at my house the other night. And you didn't get much gayer than two dads.

I poked at my egg, my sight lingering on Felix. His gaze flitted to me. Damn it. Caught again. This time, he didn't seem angry, just confused, maybe.

I cleared my throat. "So yeah, I was thinking, if you and your folks are cool with it, I could come over this weekend to your place, and we could get the outline for our magazine sketched out and ready to hand in on Monday."

"*No!*" Felix snapped, nearly taking off my head.

"Wow, okay, well, you can come over to my house then. Let me check with the dads. They tend to cram a lot into September because they're gone from October to April or beyond."

"Fine, yes, ask your fathers. I'll order from here and have it delivered." He said it as if that were the final word on everything. Which it kind of was. For now.

I had all kinds of questions that needed answering about Felix Maxwell-Sinclair.

## Chapter Ten

### Felix

EVERYTHING WOUND UP AROUND NINE, AND I HEADED out at top speed before anyone at the table could talk to me outside the small social event I'd barely made my entire way through.

Soren was trapped behind a chair, so that was one down, but Tyler was hot on my heels and caught me as I rounded the bend outside the restaurant.

"Felix?" he asked in his stupidly quiet voice and attempted to catch my arm to stop me walking.

I whirled on him, satisfied when he stumbled a step back. He glanced around him, and yeah, it was just me and him, so if he thought he was okay here, he was wrong. I didn't need Jonah and Miles backing me up to show the kid that he needed to leave me the hell alone. "What?"

"I wanted to say," he cleared his throat and mumbled something.

"I can't hear you."

"I have the entire season of *Kingston Greens* on DVD, with the extended scenes. Mom got them for me, all the way from... look, if you wanted to... next time, I'm at your place, maybe we could... together I mean."

Red rag. Bull. I stalked toward him, until his back hit the wall, and there was nowhere to move. He stumbled, and I gripped his arm to hold him, and yeah, I shook him because he needed to know I was being real here. I couldn't get his mom to stop sniffing around my dad, but I could sure as hell break them up through Tyler.

"You don't get happiness with my dad! If your mom takes one step in our house again, I'll call the cops and—"

"No!" Tyler shouted in my face, his eyes wide as he realized he'd shouted at me, and then, Soren was there, extricating Tyler, and standing between me and him.

"What is your problem, Sinclair?" Soren snapped at me.

*You!* I wanted to shout. *You're my freaking problem! Inviting me out to eat, and accusing me of hating on queer things, and being so nice, and then confusing the hell out of me! You are the problem Soren Madsen-Rowe with your perfect house, and your two perfect dads, and a little brother who adores you, and a sister who clings to you like you deserve it.*

I didn't say any of that, peering around Soren at Tyler whose eyes were bright. I probably made him cry—jeez, if all it takes is me warning him and his mom off to make the kid cry, then that was just pathetic.

No one sees *me* crying over the shit in my life.

I stared at Soren, all of us in the pool of light from the side window of the flower place. "Whatever," I snarled.

"Tyler, go back inside," Soren murmured, and Tyler left immediately.

"Awww, look at you rescuing your little boyfriend from big bad Felix." My brain wasn't connecting to my mouth properly. "Hundred to one, you get a blow job out of that."

Soren's eyes narrowed, and he stepped closer. Now, it was me up against the wall, with him caging me there. He wasn't bigger than me, or faster, but there was something deadly in his expression. Maybe, it was a glimpse of the boy he'd been before he'd lucked out with his millionaire dads. Who knew?

"Leave Tyler alone," he warned.

"Or what?" Jeez, I sounded about five. I tilted my chin, and acted like him going all big guy on campus didn't touch me. Even if it did.

"You don't want to push me," he added, and crowded even closer.

"You don't scare me."

He laughed, but it was a nasty sound, a sneer almost. "Tell that to the guy who once tried to take my kid brother's jacket. He ended up plenty scared, and he was way bigger than you."

"Whatever," I snapped.

He shook his head. "Do us both a favor, and leave Tyler alone."

"Or you'll sic your daddies on me? What are the fairies gonna do to me?"

His jaw tightened, and I saw murder in his eyes, and I readied myself for the punch—anticipating the burn as he hit my face, the blood, the high of feeling something real. He stepped back and away, brushing my jacket as if he'd found fluff on it.

"You're not worth it, Felix."

"Says the dumpster trash with the shirt-lifting dads." I pushed all my self-hatred into that sentence and expected him to lose his shit for real, but all he did was grin.

Only it was feral, and his eyes were dark with emotion. "You sat at my dads' table, and you loved every minute of it, and, not once, did you call them on being married, or together. You're full of shit. Actually, you're not even full of shit, you're nothing but an empty shell."

"Fuck you," I snapped, hating that I couldn't deny a single thing. He was right—there wasn't anything good in me—otherwise, I'd be the one with the parents who cared. I'd be the one who had friends who rushed to my defense like he did to Tyler.

He stepped fully away then, as the rest of the group came toward us, Tyler in the center, and I was done with all of it.

I left, and as soon as I was around the next corner and heading home, I broke into a jog, then a run, and the few miles until I could stop to call for a ride was nothing as I pounded the sidewalk and darted around anyone in my way. I was pissed and confused as hell when I started, but by the time Rick picked me up and dropped me back at the house, I was just plain winded and hot.

Still, it didn't take long for my breathing to settle, and I grabbed a shower, unable to think about anything like sleeping, and headed to the media room, which was about the only room in the house in which I felt calm. In the media room—with its huge screen and all the latest shows and movies to hand --, all I ever needed to do when Mom was here was turn up the volume to drown out any arguing, and if it was loud enough, no one came in to talk to me.

Win/win.

"You're back late," Dad said from behind me, and I hated that I hadn't heard him coming, or that I hadn't shut that particular door. I continued to click through the TV listings, looking for what, I didn't know, but searching for something perfect to watch in order to forget everything, was at least familiar.

Unfamiliar was the guilt I felt for hassling Tyler, or dissing Soren's dads, who were cool and normal and everything I wanted. Unfamiliar was how I felt when Soren had peeked at me as we ate, his lips curved in a smile. Or when Tyler talked about the show we might both like. Or when I got accused of being anti-queer, or whatever shit that was. I know I'd said things; I know I'd used the F-word, but I hadn't meant it.

Had I?

I was an asshole, who didn't know what to do with himself.

And how could I be anti-queer when I had all these conflicting thoughts in my head about sex, and movie stars, and singers, and freaking Soren with his freaking smile and the light shining in his stupid eyes —his stupid, pretty, soft brown eyes.

*Pretty*? Where'd that thought come from? I sank lower in the couch, flicking through channels at such a speed I didn't even know what I was staring at. Soren had smiled at me tonight, and the smile seemed genuine, but he'd hesitated as we'd locked gazes, and I know he was expecting me to smile back, like we were friends or something. We weren't friends—I didn't do friends because they only ever wanted one thing from me, my name or my mom's money—but somewhere deep inside me, something cracked open, and I was staring back at Soren, and I had feelings.

Not hatred or self-preservation, not anger or distrust, but a flare of new emotion almost like an awareness of Soren as something different. For a moment, there was a tiny flare of hope inside me, and I hated that it made me feel so vulnerable and open.

I'd gotten turned on. Just looking at Soren made me hard, and not in the fantasy kind of way, but it was real. Soren Madsen-Rowe made me have a feeling I didn't want, almost as if I was connected to Soren in school, even as I shouted at him and was unbelievably crude about his parents.

That scared me.

I glanced up at my dad, and he smiled at me as if he cared. "Did you go somewhere after hockey? Meet with friends? How is hockey going? You're playing Hershey first, right? I have the date in my diary to—"

"I gave up hockey," I lied.

His eyes widened. "But you love hockey!"

I snorted a laugh at my dad's shock. "See? You actually believed I'd give up the only thing I'm good at? Shows how much you know your own son."

The enthusiasm in his eyes dimmed, and I waited for him to shut down and leave, but instead, he pressed a hand to his temple and sighed. "I deserve that."

Damn right, he deserved that. I could count on one hand the number of games he and Mom had attended *together* last season, so why ask about hockey tonight? Yes, he'd been to most of them on his own, but it wasn't as if he stayed around after and talked to the other parents, or did hockey parent-type things. Not that I needed that because I was fine on my own, but yeah, he could have at least tried, right?

"Felix, I get it—"

"Yeah, yeah," I interrupted, wishing he'd just leave.

"I'd like to apologize for—"

"This is how the shouting starts, Dad. You tell me you're sorry for working. I believe you until the next time Mom messes things up, and I hate on her, and you go quiet. Then, Mom shouts at me for some fucking reason, and then, everyone is fucking shouting. So, let's skip all of that, and you let Mom shout at you and cut out the middleman. I'm done here." I stood up and threw the remote on the couch, and Dad stood as well, holding out a hand to stop me from leaving.

"No cursing," Dad said, automatically.

I shrugged his hand off my arm. "You don't get to tell me not to *fucking* curse."

He winced, and I shoved him away from me.

"Felix—"

"Mom's already gone, but that still leaves you, and I want to stand on our roof and curse so hard that the cops come, and they take you away, and I get to live with Phoebe and Rick, and don't have to put up with you or that woman you brought here acting like she's my mom. I don't want you. I don't want Mom, I don't need a new one, and I just want to curse. Okay!"

He relaxed his hold on my arm, his face crumpled, and I swear he was going to cry. How was it that he got to cry?

"Felix. Please."

"No."

"I wish…" Dad pressed a hand to his chest, rubbing over his heart. "Felix, your mom was here because we were signing papers, because we're actually, *finally*, getting a divorce." His voice hitched. "I tried to keep us together, but…"

Some dark part of me took over, almost as if this evening was all about breaking me apart. First, Soren with his eyes and his smile; Tyler with his stupid DVDs; and now, Dad telling me about something that should have happened years back before the rot of their marriage landed in my lap.

"About time," I yelled with every ounce of my pent-up resentment, right in his face.

He backed up a step almost as if he was afraid of me. Was my dad afraid of me? Then, he seemed to steady himself and pulled his shoulders back. "Stop it."

"No—"

"You don't get to tell me no! I'm your father, and you will listen to me!" He retook his seat and waited, and after a pause, he sent me a cautious look. "Please, can we talk?"

This was a different dad to the one I expected. This was him actually wanting to talk to me as if we had a connection.

As if I mattered.

I sat down and waited, picking at a thread in my jeans and not liking my dad's guarded gaze one little bit.

"I meant to break it to you gently," he began, "about the divorce, I mean."

"It's all good, it was inevitable," I shrugged to underscore how much I didn't care. "I've known, since I was five, that you hated each other."

"We don't... we didn't..."

"I remember Mom wanted one of those enormous bouncy castle things in the garden for my sixth birthday. You didn't want me to have one. You shouted, Mom shouted, my birthday was ruined because none of the other kids wanted to stay."

"Six?" Dad whispered the word as if he couldn't believe it.

"Yep. Which makes nearly ten years of shitty memories. Or at least Mom did, all you did was back down, step away, and leave me right by her side."

He paused. "I *did* want you to have it."

"What?"

"The castle."

"No, you didn't. She was yelling—"

"Not at you. It was never about you."

"Shame I lived in the house then, because it sure as hell always felt as if it was about me."

"We argued because she wanted this big dramatic party, and we couldn't afford anything like that."

"Yeah right, Dad." I rolled my eyes dramatically. Now, he was just talking bullshit because Mom's family was swimming in the almighty dollar.

"No, listen…" He waited for a moment, as if he was searching for exactly the right words. "Do you remember anything about the house when you were that little?"

I recalled images of a much smaller place, a large backyard, and that there was a dog that barked next door. I knew my room had a tree right outside the window, and I'd imagined climbing down it when I was eight, to run away and live in some unnamed city. I even packed a bag with string cheese, a half-empty bottle of Coke, my lucky Captain America underwear, T-shirts, and a clean pair of jeans. How far I was expecting to get on that, I didn't know, but I did know that Phoebe had found me crying at the bottom of the garden. She'd told me that I needed more than string cheese if I was going to make it all the way to the city and offered to make me sandwiches, but I never left, not after she made me PB&J, and I fell a little in love with her.

"The place over on Magnolia," Dad prompted.

"I remember it."

"That was *our* house, mine and your mom's. We didn't use a single cent of her money from Sinclair-Staten Pharma because she didn't want to." He paused and waited for me to catch up, but what he'd said didn't make sense because Mom was all about the money. Still, I stayed quiet and waited for him to carry on. "It was idyllic, and she was my best friend. I was building my business as a broker, and she said she was happy so many times that I believed her. Then, we had you, and it was like our little family was complete." He drifted away on a sea of memories that I swear he was making up. Mom had never been happy, since the first day I could ever recall knowing that she was my mom. I waited for more, but he stared at the wall, a soft smile on his face, rubbing his chest where I assumed that these fake memories lived.

"Speed it up, Dad." He shot me a confused glance, and I felt guilty. He was still my dad, and I was being an asshole, even if I did feel justified. "How does this link to a bouncy castle?"

"Sorry, I was just thinking about that house." He smiled. "I loved that house. Anyway, we couldn't afford what she wanted for your birthday—not the castle, or the entertainers, or the fancy catering—at least, not without your mom dipping into her family money, but that was what she wanted for you." He tilted his head. "This was just after her grandpa died, and she was just about to turn twenty-eight," he paused again, and this time, something clicked. My Sinclair family trust fund kicked in at twenty-eight, so I guessed the same was true for Mom?

"We never talked about it, even when she was only weeks from having access to all that money. We'd promised, from day one, that whatever we did, would be on our own, but we were just naïve kids. Your mom told me that she'd do what *she* wanted with *her* money, and it was nothing to do with *me*. It was one of the first times that we argued, and I'm sorry you remember that."

He sent me a beseeching gaze, as if it was important that I understand, but I was stubborn, as well as stupid, and I crossed my arms over my chest. "I might not have remembered the start of it all, but the arguing never stopped from that day."

"I know."

"Do you though?"

"I can't talk for your mom…" He closed his eyes briefly as if the emotions overwhelmed him. "She wanted more than me and that small house, and I agreed with whatever she said in the end, because I loved her. She employed Phoebe as a nanny for you, even though she always said she never wanted her kids to be brought up the same way as her. I thought she was happy being with us, but I was wrong. Then, she wanted to take us all to New York, but it wasn't the three of us—we had a nanny with her husband, and this serviced apartment she'd bought in the city— and everything moved so fast."

"But we're not *in* New York," I said.

Dad sighed, rubbing his chest again, his lips thinning. "Only because I fought for us to have a normal life, and I didn't want us sucked into the toxic Sinclair drama."

"But all their money? We could have…" I didn't know how to finish that.

"Yeah, all their money that rots them from the inside," Dad muttered. "This place was the compromise."

"It was?" I glanced out of the door to the hallway beyond with the chandelier and the marble flooring. If this was a compromise on using Sinclair wealth, then it still involved their money.

"I didn't want you moved. You were happy at school, and you had friends, but then, she was so unhappy, and you were changing, becoming hard, listening to us fight, the way she would…"

"Scream at you? Use me as a bargaining chip? So, what you're saying is that all of this is Mom's fault? I don't think it all falls on her, Dad. You might not have argued back most of the time, but you were never here, and you messed up your fair share of times—"

He held out a hand as if he was imploring me to listen. "You're right, this isn't all on your mom. This is on me, as well, for demanding to do what I thought was right for you. I was so tired of what was happening that you ended up with nothing. Everything should have been for you, and you were the one person we let down. And now look at you— you're so angry all the time. I'm sorry."

"Is that it?" I asked after a short pause.

Dad frowned. "I love you, and I want us to be—"

"No!" I interrupted. "You tell me that you and Mom messed up, and now you're what, a new man? Did Mom threaten to cut you off from her money? Is that why you want me to chill, so you can get to mine? Did Mom find out you were sleeping with Lilly Corrigan?"

He sighed. "Oh, Felix, no. I'm not sleeping with Lilly—"

"Are you replacing me with her son because he's better than me? Not as damaged or whatever?" It was like ripping skin off to ask that question.

His sad expression was chased away by horror. "What? No! Jeez, Felix, no. They needed somewhere to stay. They were in one of the guest rooms."

"If you say so."

"I was helping Lilly and her son. She needed help… a friend." He seemed so old right then, silver at his temples, even though he was only forty-seven, his face lined, and his eyes bright with emotion.

"I'm not stupid. It's obvious what you're doing."

"I know you're not stupid, and I wish I could tell you everything, but it's not my story to tell. Felix, she and her boy need friends like us now. If you and Tyler could be friends—"

"I have friends. I don't need another one, especially a queer like him," I snorted.

"That's enough!" Dad snapped. "I don't want to hear you saying things like that. He's a good kid."

"Whatever Dad. Are we done? There's a divorce; you're okay, I'm not okay, and now, I'm going to bed." I pushed past him, and he tried to catch my arm, but I was faster, and I was up in my room with the door locked, right in front of my Ten poster. He was standing there, looking down at me, smiling. I bet *he* never lied to Soren. I bet it was all freaking perfect in their house. I ripped the poster off the wall in one tear, then the others, each an image of my heroes, and I tore them into the tiniest of pieces.

I even felt a bit better, for a moment.

And, then, I just felt like shit.

## Chapter Eleven

### Soren

THINGS WERE WEIRD OVER THE NEXT WEEK OR SO.

Weird with Felix, which, hey, it was Felix, so I expected things to be antagonistic, which they were… sort of, but not as much? Yeah, it was messing with my head. Like, there were days or times, I'd say something, or he would, and we'd have, like, a moment. Not like a movie moment where we would stare into each other's dewy eyes, then proclaim undying love. I mean, seriously, no. But times, like today, during our first team scrimmage. Coach—like every other adult human being in my life—had suddenly decided that Soren/Felix was the best pairing since Ash and Pikachu. Seemed, we were always on the same line, same scrimmage team, same classes, same house. Maybe, the gods were trying to teach me something. What that was, I had no effing clue. So far, the only lesson I was getting was in patience, because Felix Maxwell-Sinclair tried mine at every opportunity. Until he wasn't...

Head space, total chalk.

Today, he was being okay. Not exactly Mr. Sunshine, but okay. Tomorrow, he might show up and be the largest penis in a Chesterford jacket you ever met. Maybe, that not knowing what to expect was what was making me so edgy and unsettled. Not the pink of his lips or the flecks of darker blue in his eyes. Nope. None of those things. Those were movie moments. And right now, Felix and I were not in any way Nick and Charlie from *Heartstopper.* At the moment, we were more Andi and April from *Parks and Recreation,* minus the married stuff.

The first half of the scrimmage was just us working out the kinks after a long summer and trying to find some cohesion. Felix and I were on the white team, the players divvied up equally. Tyler was on our side, which totally did not add any drama to the situation. Not. The tension in Felix, around Tyler, was so thick you could smear it on your toast and skip the peanut butter and honey.

They actually played well together. Tyler was fast with soft hands, and Felix was good at picking up his passes. We won the game, such as it was, and then, spent the other half of the practice working on special teams, with attention to playing short-handed, something that had given us trouble last season. We didn't suck, but we could certainly be better with our penalty kills. Too many goals given up and that sort of thing. I was out on the ice with three forwards on this round, the last time we'd been two and two, with a duo of forwards and a duo of defensemen.

A volunteer coach acted as a ref, and Coach Sennett was sitting up in the high seats taking notes. I didn't mind playing a D-man. Coach liked us to know how to cover all the positions. Made us well-rounded, he said. During a PK drill—and sometimes in games, if someone was hurt—we had to be ready to play all the possible angles. The forwards were good, don't get me wrong, but they didn't have the mindset that was drummed into the heads of defensive players. Living with a defensive coach, I'd had all kinds of knowledge passed along.

They kind of floated at times, when they should have been keeping a good defensive position between themselves and the shooter. And being outnumbered 5-4 made it hard to get into a slot in front of the net, as I normally would, because I had to move steadily to follow the passes the opposing team was making. Shaun was on the other team, and he was a threat. Our captain had a brutal wrist shot. He liked to park himself on the left side of the net and get off a one-timer that travelled at Mach ten. No shit, the puck would break the sound barrier. We should call Shaun *Maverick*. He and Tom Cruise going supersonic while 'Danger Zone' plays in the background.

The red jerseys were all set up with Shaun in his office. I was trying to cover my man on the far side of the net, when Shaun let one rip. Felix—in a decidedly un-Felix like move—threw himself in front of the puck to block the shot. It worked. The puck deflected off his calf to me, and I dumped it out of our zone as Felix went down to his knee, his face a mask of hurt. I skated over as he pushed hot, fast breaths in and out, spittle flying, while struggling to work through the pain.

"Great block," I said, then offered him my hand as a whistle was blown, and the volunteer coach, Gavin Neeley's dad, came over to check on Felix. Indecisive blue eyes flicked to my hand, then up to my face. I smiled down at him. Felix, then, slapped his sweaty glove into my sweaty glove, and let me hoist him to his skates.

"You okay?" Mr. Neeley asked as the others began to gather around us mumbling compliments about the shot block.

"Yeah, just hurts," Felix replied, his face still tight with pain. Yeah, it hurt big time. I had bruises all season long from diving in front of frozen chunks of rubber flying at me at ninety or so miles per hour.

"That was gutsy," Tyler stated, and we all nodded. Stepping in front of one of Shaun's wristers was like leaping in front of a brick fired out of an air cannon.

"Yeah, nice block," Shaun said, then clapped Felix on the shoulder.

Felix nodded, grimacing, but I thought I saw maybe a tweak of one corner of his mouth. Hard to say with the mask and mouthguard, but just maybe, he was a little happy.

Coach called the scrimmage, then, and we headed off the ice; Felix hobbling along. I glanced back, saw him behind us, and waited for him to exit the ice.

"I know where the locker room is," Felix sniped as he gimped onto the rubber padding leading from the ice to the Coyote dressing room.

"You sure? I know you're not the brightest bulb in the chandelier," I replied and got a nudge in the side so hard it made me gasp.

"How old are you? Like a hundred and two? Who

says things like that?" He parried as I rubbed my side playfully, or pretended it was playful. Felix was pretty strong to be honest.

"My grandparents are over for a few days. The parental units are down in Charlotte for a preseason game. My grandfather says dorky things like that all the time. Guess it rubbed off."

He studied me for a quick second. "Oh, well, that's cool that your grandpa's cheesy."

And off he went, favoring his right leg, as I stood there all primed for a nasty elitist comeback and not getting one. Huh. That was…weird. Like I said, everything was weird AF right now.

---

"Hey Slick!" Gramps called as I climbed into his green SUV while "Mack the Knife" rolled out of the speakers. Several kids' heads turned. My face got hot. "You look overexerted. Did Coach Sennett work you hard today?"

"Yeah, he did," I covered, then reached over to turn down the music. Gramps loved the crooners. Guys like Frank Sinatra, Bing Crosby, Perry Como. Those guys. Which was cool. Hearing those songs gave me a wider enjoyment of music. Eclectic, as Ten would say. Gramps, also, liked to sing along to all the old songs really loudly. Grandma said she thought he was going deaf, but Gramps denied that vehemently. I paused as the aroma of pizza hit my nose. Peeking into the back seat, I saw three pizza boxes and pumped the air. We didn't get pizza a lot at home. Living with professional athletes in season meant tons of healthy food. "Did Grandma go somewhere?" I asked because Grandma also liked to feed us kids lots of green stuff.

"She's not gone anywhere; she's just tired from doing her aerobic walking class. I think her psychotic nerve is acting up, but she won't admit that." He pulled away from the school, the grounds quiet now as classes had let out hours ago.

"Sciatic," I corrected, then snickered.

"Right." Gramps grinned. He looked a lot like his sons. Or, I guess, his sons resembled him. Tall, lean, with dark hair and hazel eyes. You could look at my grandfather and see my dad Ten in about thirty years. Silver threaded through his hair, and laugh lines at the corners of his eyes and mouth. "So, here's something that I learned today. Did you know that Linda from the garden center has a granddaughter who plays field hockey?"

"Gramps…"

"What? Is there a law against talking to a friend over the mulch bags about our grandkids?"

"No, there's no law, but I'm not really looking to date right now." That was a total lie. If I met the right person, I would be all over dating them. I was fifteen years old. My body was all about dating. And other things of a physical nature that went along with dating. I was more than ready to burn my V card, but I wanted it to be with someone special. "I'm trying to focus on my studies and hockey."

"You can study with a pretty girl or guy. Just saying. And Tiffany is a junior. An older woman. Wink. Wink."

"Dude, honestly, if Grandma heard you saying that, she would come unglued," I chuckled as we left the campus behind, while Vic Damone sang about having an affair to remember. The fact that I knew it was Vic Damone was cool and scary all at once. "I'll pass on Tiffany, but thanks for looking out for my dismal dating status."

"If you change your mind, just let me know. I'm going to get your father's flower beds mulched for winter, so I'll probably be running back to the garden center a few times."

I nodded, but knew I'd not be asking Linda's granddaughter out any time soon. I disliked blind dates, and right now, I wasn't looking for romance. Not that I didn't want a date for the Halloween dance, obvs, but not with some girl I'd never met. Maybe, Courtney and I would end up going together. We did last year a few times, just as friends. Yeah, maybe I'd ask her now and get that social monkey off my back.

---

"SOREN, YOU SHOULD HAVE SAID SOMETHING LIKE A week ago," Courtney said as we worked on graphics for my Twitch channel later that night. She was in her place; I was in mine—thank god for video.

"Sooner? The dance is a month away. Like, that's a lifetime." I sat back to stare at her face in the tiny corner of my monitor.

"Well, yeah, normally, but Sid and Meghan just broke up, and I saw my chance, so I took it." She grinned while adding some blood to the promo lettering for our Halloween Horror Game Fest running through the month of October.

"Who the hell is Sid?" I asked, then took a sip of grape soda.

"He's the captain of the varsity swim team." She gave me a smug little smirky smirk.

"Captain? So, he's a senior?"

She made a face, then threw her hands over the camera atop her monitor. "Would you be quiet!?"

"Your mom doesn't know he's older?" I whispered, leaning up to get my lips close to my microphone, while Court hurried to plug her headphones in. Mrs. Barnes had some pretty tight rules for her only child when it came to dating, makeup, and social outings.

"No, and she's not to find out. Sid is so gorgeous. Remember that Thai BL about the swim team members?" Like I could forget. Hashtag anime nosebleed. "Well, he's built like that." She fanned herself, and I had to laugh.

"Good luck. You better hope your mother doesn't find out, or you'll be grounded until you graduate college." I glanced at the time on my screen. "I have to roll. Felix and I are meeting at the library at eight to interview Desmond the janitor."

"That sounds horrible. He always smells like old peanuts." She shuddered theatrically. "Have fun. Hey, if worse comes to worst, you could always ask Felix!"

She exited before I could fire back a volley. So, I did it in a text with numerous middle finger emojis. I got a line of laughing tear-faced emojis and eggplant emojis back.

I grabbed my books and phone, stuffed them into

my backpack, and went downstairs to inform my grandparents that I was heading to the library to study with a guy. Not a friend, not a buddy, just a guy. Gramps still gave me a wink and twenty bucks, then went back to his viewing of *Columbo*.

"Let me know when you get there," Grandma said as she looked up from her knitting lesson. Lottie was obsessed with learning how to make hats so she could give them to the lawn fairies living in the backyard. She was big into fairies this week, which explained her Tinkerbell nightgown and the floppy yellow nylon wings she was wearing. "And be home by eleven. It's a school night."

"Yep, will do!" I called, taking the twenty and cramming it into my front pocket, then jogging down the steps to the corner. Soon, I'd be old enough to get my learner's permit. Then, I could use my savings for a car and be freed from having to ride city buses or having my grandfather pick me up after practices. I mean, I didn't mind the bus—usually—or being picked up, but…okay, I did. I wanted to drive. To go where I wanted, when I wanted, with no one riding shotgun or preaching to me about the horrors of lens wipes like that dude on the bus two weeks ago. I wasn't sure lens wipes were the root of all evil, but he was damned adamant about it. My dads said they'd match everything I saved, and I had my eye on a few cars that weren't selling close by.

One day…

———

THE MARY B. BILLOWS LIBRARY WAS AN OLD building, one of many on the Chesterford campus. Lots of gray stone, iron works on the patios, and loads of *Hamilton* vibes with musty oils on the walls, stone fireplaces, and that dusty old book smell. It was open until 7 on Tuesdays and Thursdays, so we had about an hour before we were chased out. Felix was seated at a table under the portrait of a Revolutionary war-era lady with a daring amount of décolletage and a severe frown. He was deep into whatever he was reading and didn't hear me creeping up. I slapped a hand to his shoulder, and he leapt about a foot.

"Fucker," he spat and got a glower and a hush from the librarian placing books back on the shelves.

I snickered under my breath and dumped my bag on the table with a thud, which got me another dark glower from the librarian. I ducked my head, hair falling into my face to hide me, and kicked Felix gently under the table. He winced.

"Oh sorry. How's the bruise?" I asked in a

whisper. An older man was sitting across from us reading a newspaper, and I thought only my grandfather read paper newspapers.

"It was feeling better until you kicked it," he growled softly.

"Oops. So, what have you gotten?"

He spun the book he had been reading around, then pointed at an image. "This is from a book about the Vietnam War. Do you recognize this man?" He tapped the blurry image. I studied it hard. The picture was grainy; the men all looking sapped and sore, and tired beyond any extreme. "This is a picture of Desmond Parks. And this is, also, Desmond." He tapped another image on the next page, the same Black man we knew, only older. Marching down the street in a military uniform and waving a small American flag. "He served in the Vietnam War, then went on to be a vocal part of a veterans' group trying to fix the disparities shown to Black soldiers in Vietnam."

"Wow," I whispered, awed to think that this man we saw scraping gum from under desks and mopping up spills in the bathrooms had been so awesome. "I bet he has a lot of powerful stories to tell us."

He glanced up, blue eyes rich with something I didn't quite understand, but really liked seeing. His gaze dropped to my mouth. I sort of moved in as he did, arms on the table, legs pushing our butts from our chairs a few inches and...

Someone called his name. His eyes left mine. I glanced over my shoulder to see Desmond limping in, looking nothing like a janitor. Gone were the overalls and mop. Today, he was just in jeans and an old tee with a local chicken shack logo on the front.

We stood, suddenly feeling as if we should do more than sit there and gawk. He stopped dead to study us, as if he feared we were going to pelt him with water balloons.

"Mr. Parks. Thank you for coming to talk with us," I said, wondering if I should salute or something. I didn't, but it felt like I should. This man had served our country in a terrible war. "Sit down. We were just looking through some old books."

"Ah, I remember that one. The author asked for images from the men in my regiment. Then, we struck up a friendship, so when he wanted to tackle the injustices that Black men faced in that war, he looked me up. We still talk to this day," Desmond said as he eased himself into a seat. "I have to say, I'm shocked you two kids want to talk to me."

We sat back down. Felix pulled out his phone to record the interview. "We're doing a magazine project about the history of Chesterford, and you're one of the most interesting people we've discovered so far. You marched for veterans' rights way back in the eighties. Tell us what that was about," I said and got a nod from Felix.

"Well, a group of Black veterans wanted to bring a few things to Congress' attention. So we gathered, and we marched. See, back in the war, things weren't segregated, but they sure weren't equal…"

We sat there for an hour listening to Desmond talk and asking questions. The librarian finally escorted us out, the lights dimming as soon as the door was locked behind us.

"Thank you, Mr. Parks. This is…. well, this is really amazing. You've lived through so much and done so many cool things. Thanks for sitting down with us," Felix said.

I bobbed my head in agreement. Desmond shook both of our hands, then slowly made his way out of the door.

"That was way cooler than I thought it would be," I said.

"Yeah, it was." He smiled so hard, and right then I wanted to tug him closer and taste the smile—kiss him until he kissed me back.

*Stop with thinking about kissing.*

I changed the subject as Felix stared at me curiously. God, I hope he couldn't read minds. "I should talk to my grandfather about his time in the war. He rarely talks about serving, but I know he did. What about your family?"

He seemed to stiffen then, the smiling and relaxed Felix melting away to reveal the snippy one I knew far too well. And that made me sad because the smiling Felix was so much nicer to be around.

"What do you care about my family? Why are you always so damned nosy?" His voice was loud, echoing in the small lobby.

"Dude, chill the hell out. You're like this freaking Jekyll and Hyde. I think I see the real you, but then some other monster rears up and snaps off my head. I'm not sure who the real Felix is, but you really need to learn to be better. I'm doing my best to be a friend, but—"

Tyler walked out of the side entrance to the library, his arms filled with books. Felix ran off after him, leaving me to stew alone. Whatever. I was so over the drama with him.

## Chapter Twelve

### Felix

I DON'T KNOW WHAT COMPELLED ME TO GO AFTER Tyler. I could have called his name, but that would mean he got a heads-up that I was heading his way, and I'd end up scaring him. Instead, I followed him outside. He'd held the door open for me, not realizing it was me he was holding it open for, and then, when he did, he'd stumbled back and nearly fell down the three steps. I caught him at the last moment, my fingers circling his wrist.

"Leave me alone," he attempted to yank his hand free, and once I was sure he was steady, I let him go, but I was now between him and the steps, so he could either go back through the door into the library, or do what he usually did when no one was around to help him, and stand there like a startled deer.

"I just want to talk to you," I said, and when he shrunk down, I realized I'd defaulted to my intimidating voice, and I didn't know what the hell I was doing.

"You need some help with girly-queer here?" Miles said from behind me, his expression mean. What in god's name was Miles doing anywhere near a damn library? I glanced over at him, and beyond to the large group of guys he'd separated away from. They all looked like him, jeans, white T-shirts, and buzzed hair. It was like they'd traveled in a herd.

"I don't need your help!" I snapped.

Miles immediately backed up, then away, the big guy cowed by me shouting at him. Tyler stared at me with wide glassy eyes, a hint of kohl at each corner, as he pushed his long, pink-tinged bangs back from his face. He was a hockey player, fast on his skates—more the kind to outrun a problem, than be in a huddle waiting to get hurt—and our team needed his skills as being quick and kind of wiry, but it had never occurred to me that he wasn't that much smaller than me, and solid. It was the soft pink tinge to his hair, and the quiet way he spoke, and how he smiled with such innocence that meant he seemed frailer than he actually was.

Also, the way I managed to scare him since his mom had been in our kitchen. I'd lashed out—like a kid having a tantrum—and Tyler deserved better than that.

If he'd been a bigger guy than me, or worse, *richer*, would I have felt okay pushing him into a locker? Would I have let my parents get into my head so much that I could punish him for what *his* mom might be doing with *my* dad?

"Is that what you call me? Girly-queer, I mean." Tyler asked in such a quiet voice that I had to strain to listen.

"No," I defended, and he stared at me, and I couldn't lie because he had some weird power over me. "Yes."

He tipped his chin. "And that's the best you could come up with," he murmured, probably thinking I wouldn't hear. Then, he dropped his bag to the ground opened his shaking hands, palm up, and closed his eyes. "Just do it already."

"What?"

He half opened one eye. "I'm guessing you want to hit me. Or shout at me, or do any of a million things that make you feel better?" He was trembling, and seemed defeated, like he couldn't even muster up the energy to even be afraid. "I give up. I'm done."

"I only want to talk." I backed up a couple more steps, bumping into a wooden bench by a table, and, as if my strings had been cut, I slumped to the bench. I didn't understand what was happening in my head, what Soren's words had started inside me, or maybe, it was Dad saying Tyler needed friends, and me pretending I had friends. I didn't have any friends; hell, Soren was about the closest I came to anything like one, and how freaking sad was that? All I had was Jonah and Miles, who followed me around and did what I said and reinforced my position in school as someone who mattered just because of their money.

Did I actually matter at all? What mark was I going to leave on this school apart from people at reunions recalling one of the many rich kids who thought it was okay to shout and threaten and intimidate? And the reason all of this occurred to me had to be because of my parents divorcing, and nothing to do with Soren Madsen-Rowe.

Who was I kidding—I'd known the divorce was inevitable, and I'd already worked through the expectations—it was Soren who was the problem. Soren was forcing me, one cautious push at a time, to connect with him. The connection had turned to confusion and me being constantly turned on, and realizing I was gay, and that I needed to stop and think about things. No one in the Sinclair family was openly queer, so where did I fit in with my mom's side of the family? She already hated Dad—what if she ended up hating me, too?

Tyler hesitated for a moment, picking up his bag and, cautiously, rounding the table, but not sitting down. He vibrated with nervous anticipation, and I'd done that to him, worn him down until he was nervous to even sit opposite me. Soren was right when he wondered who the real me was, and just as right to tell me that I had everything in me to be better. I wasn't anything real at all, and I would go further than that, I was a mess—a broken asshole who didn't even have a heart, yet expected the world to bend to me. I was the worst kind of person, and I was sad, and impossibly lonely, and as pathetic as my dad.

"You can sit down if you want," I said, even if it would be easier if he stood there as I said my piece and, then, left.

"Why?" He opened his eyes fully and glanced around him, as if he expected Miles to come back, or for Jonah to appear, or maybe for me to launch over the table and pin him to a wall.

"I want to talk."

"What about?" He frowned as he fiddled with the snap of his backpack. I focused in on the rainbow pin attached to a pocket, and the colors blurred. He was clearly out, always had been as far as I recall, with his rainbow pins and the faint color in his hair and the hint of kohl that was definitely not in adherence to school guidelines. But somehow, he got away with it. Was the smudge of dark gray around his eyes there because he'd used makeup this morning? Or was it left over from last night? I could imagine him sitting in front of a mirror applying colors, maybe videoing it for social media, and messing with his hair, and feeling right in his own body... maybe...

"What are you?" Hell; that was the most garbled nonsense ever. *What are you? Where did that even come from?* My face burned with humiliation, and I almost got up and left before Tyler saw my weakness.

"What am I?" Tyler asked, confused. "Studying? No? Human, maybe. Is that what you meant?"

"No. Are you, I mean, do you do *that* a lot?" I waved at him, more specifically his face.

"What?" Tyler's frown deepened, and he dipped his head so his bangs fell forward to hide his delicate features again.

"The makeup. I mean it looks good on your eyes,

smoky. Not that I'd wear it because I'd end up looking like someone from Kiss, and my hands aren't that steady." I held out a hand and fake-shook it. "See?"

His head shot up. "Are you messing with me?" Again, he glanced around, then stared back at me with suspicion. "What is this? Lull me into chatting, and then what, you're gonna leap over the table and pummel me?" He tipped his chin again. "Hurry up with whatever you're doing because I promised mom I'd be back before dark."

"No, I genuinely... look... Soren said I was... no, I'm saying that I need to..." I stopped because that was just a garbled mess of nothing, and all it did was confuse Tyler, who appeared to either be waiting for a punchline or for me to punch him. Why was this sincerity shit so hard? "My dad said you needed a friend."

He winced. "What?"

"He said you and your mom were at the house that morning because you needed friends."

"And that's *all* he told you?" Tyler rubbed at his arm and looked like he might bolt.

My heart sank, had Dad been lying? For some insane reason, I imagined my dad had been honest with me. "Was Dad lying? Are your mom and him—"

The door slammed and Soren stepped out, seeing me and Tyler together, and standing there like some kind of avenging angel. "What's going on!" he demanded, and jumped the three steps to loom over me. "Are you okay, Tyler? Jesus, Felix, just when I think you might have a freaking heart, you shove yourself on Tyler again. If you have something to say—"

"We're talking," I interrupted whatever Soren was going to throw at me.

He eyed me with suspicion. "Talking?" he asked, his anger subsiding, and his narrowed gaze moving from Tyler to me and back again.

"Yeah, you know, where people open their mouths and words come out." I couldn't resist one jab.

"What did you do to Tyler?" He demanded.

"Nothing," I said quietly.

"He says he wants to talk to me." Tyler sounded as if he might be in shock.

He and Soren exchanged glances and, then, Soren immediately sat opposite me with a concerned expression.

I lost myself in Soren's eyes. The color of them, the way they lit with his smile or darkened in defensiveness, the way they'd gone all soft when we were talking in the library. What would he do if I reached over the table and yanked him toward me and kissed him, or something more stupid, like tell him I wanted to kiss him first?

"So, talk," Soren's tone was nothing like how he'd talked to me in the library. This wasn't all tender words of understanding; this was Soren being there for Tyler—for the friend I'd lost my shit with all because his mom was…

What? Close with my dad? More? Even if they were more, then what did it matter? Mom was gone, one visit in forever, and that was just to sign papers, shout at my dad, and threaten to take me away. Their marriage was over.

I tore my gaze from Soren and stared at Tyler, who paused, then moved so he straddled the bench next to Soren. If this wasn't a serious thing— whatever the thing was—I might have laughed at the interview type set-up they had going on, Tyler confused and Soren acting as if I was a bomb ready to explode.

"What else should my dad have told me?" I asked Tyler.

He glanced away, and paused for so long that I thought he wasn't going to answer, but then, he looked back at me. "My mom likes your dad," Tyler began, and I stiffened, because this was the moment he said that my dad had been lying and Tyler's mom was sleeping with my dad. "They're friends." His eyes brightened with emotion. "I'm glad she has a friend like the ones I have." He bumped shoulders with Soren, who threw a smile at Tyler. The same beautiful smile that I'd been noticing way too much recently.

"So, wait, they're not... y'know..." I waggled my finger, but god knows what that would convey; also, I hated myself for asking.

He gasped. "No. Well... I don't know... Right now, she just needs someone to listen, and somewhere safe for us to be if we need it." He caught himself as if he'd said something he shouldn't.

"Why do you *need* to be safe?" I asked, but that was Tyler's cue to shut down, and he shouldered his backpack.

"We're done here," he said, and left at a jog, and I was bewildered by the way he'd ended the conversation so suddenly.

"I never even got to say I'd like to try to be his friend," I said, and only after the words slipped out did I recall Soren was sitting *right there.*

He stared at me; his mouth open. "Huh?"

I scrambled to stand, and ignoring him, I headed

for the front of the school where Rick would be to pick me up, with Soren right by my side.

"What was all that with Tyler?" Soren asked maybe two or three times, stopping as I reached Rick in the car.

I rounded on him and poked his chest. "Get out of my face."

He watched me leave, his hands forced into his pockets, and I refused to acknowledge him.

"Good day?" Rick asked.

"Yeah," I lied.

I was super good at lying.

## Chapter Thirteen

### Soren

THERE WAS THIS REALLY OLD METAL SONG—LIKE SO old that my dad Ten rocked out to it—that screamed about *getting down with the sickness*.

Pretty good tune to be honest. I actually had it on a playlist with all my other eclectic music. If I could take that song and change the lyrics to fit my life, it would be *to get down with the weirdness* for the weirdness had grown exponentially. And not being Wednesday Addams, I wasn't totally at ease living in the weirdness. Things I thought had been set in stone were now piles of rubble at my feet.

Felix and I had definitely had a movie moment in the library. And not like a cool movie moment where, like, a red balloon floats by and some kid comes face-to-face with a demented clown/creepy charred dead kid in the basement. Nope, to be honest, given how my gut now cramped and my skin flushed every time I saw Felix, I'd rather face the dead charred kid. Okay, maybe not, but damn, things were screwed up. What had even led me to want to kiss Felix? Hadn't I hated him like a month ago?

*Yes, yes, I had.*

Shit. I shook off that rom-com scene starring me and Felix under the painting of the frowning Revolutionary War lady, or the almost desperate need to kiss him in the library lobby.

Music and kissing aside, this was not the time to space out. We were playing our first game against Hershey. Everyone was here. My dads, grandparents, and siblings, and all the parents of all the players. Even Tyler's mom and Felix's dad, who were sitting side by side, sharing a blanket and a thermos of hot coffee and cheering.

It was surreal that everyone was acting as though nothing had changed when everything *had* changed. I'd almost kissed Felix. Twice. And he hadn't shied away that first time, or drawn back. He had leaned in, over the books about Black war veterans and sheafs of scribbled notes. He'd gotten that glazed look in those sky-blue eyes and moved closer. Why? Was he being a dick? Was he waiting for our lips to be super close then pulling back to call me a stupid queer? Were his knuckle-dragging buddies hiding in the non-fiction section ready to take videos when he shredded me for trying to make a move? Why was I so stupid to fall for a straight guy who wore his asshole badge proudly? There were, literally, two hundred or so people to crush on at Chesterford. Millions all over the world. And I pick the school's biggest dick. What did that say about me? It said I was a dumbass.

"Heads up!" Coach shouted as a puck flew into the bench area.

We all ducked, me a fraction of an inch slower because of my head being in the clouds. Coach caught the puck, then chucked it to the linesman. Nice reflexes for an old guy. I chanced a look down the bench to find Felix staring out at the action, his mouthguard hanging from one corner of his mouth, his cheeks pink from exertion. He was stupid-gorgeous. I mean, the kind of pretty that made you stupid. Me. Made *me* stupid. "Rowe. You planning on joining your line out there?"

I jerked when Coach tapped me on the helmet. "Sorry Coach," I mumbled, then threw my legs over the boards, my face red hot with embarrassment. I had to shake free from this headspace. Ten and Jared had finagled their way clear to see this game before they had to leave for a short road trip down south to start the new NHL season. Also, we just really wanted to start the season off with a win.

*Right. Head in the game, Soren.*

Knowing that Hershey was a mediocre team, I kind of sailed through their defensive line after a faceoff win. Hershey had lost a lot of their better defensemen to the varsity team over the summer, so the majority of D-men they had on the ice were frosh. That gave us an edge we'd been using to our advantage so far. Our first fifteen-minute period had seen us grab two goals to their none. The second period, they'd come out with a bit more jump, and snuck one past our goalie to get them within one. Now, with six minutes left, we were still in the lead, but looking for another goal to give us some breathing room. The ice was not great. Patches were a little rutty and soft, which meant a lot of players were going down for seemingly no reason. Passing the puck was becoming interesting.

I shuttled a fast pass to Caleb, our center man, and watched in horror as it hit a slurry spot on the ice, slowing it down just enough for a Hershey defender to get a stick on it. Cussing to myself, I had to hit the afterburners to try to catch the guy with the puck as he raced at our goal. Knowing I'd fucked up, I did what anyone would do to save themselves. I stuffed my stick into the puck carrier's skates and took him down. Whistles blew as the dude who had been about to get a quality shot on goal slid headfirst into our net. He was fine, mad, and searching for blood when he got to his skates. I was already on my way to the penalty box without even being told to go. I knew I'd get a lecture from Coach for the giveaway. No matter the ice conditions, that was totally on me.

I spat my mouthguard into my gloved hand and took the offered water bottle from the penalty box official, a volunteer from the booster club. Caleb's dad gave me a look of commiseration. He'd known I had done what needed doing. The next two minutes were tense, with several quality shots on our goal, but none of them got past Cullen. Thank all the hockey gods.

I hit the ice like a rocket, skating hard into the play, lifting the stick of one of the Hershey players to steal the puck. This time, I passed it cleanly, the puck sailing to Felix who rifled a shot at the Hershey net that clanged loudly off the crossbar. The home crowd groaned.

I made my way to the bench, hoping to not get

gnawed on too badly by Coach. He gave me a look, the kind of look that singed my balls a little. Not going to lie.

When the buzzer sounded, the Coyote fans and backers all rose and howled along with us on the bench. That was our way of celebrating wins. Head back howls and yips. After the celebratory howls, we shook hands with the other team, then, filled with energy, made our way to the locker room. Coach came in to give us a little pep talk and point out things we needed to do better next game. Overall, he went pretty light on me, so later, I felt good leaving the locker room to meet the family and boosters at the local pizza parlor.

The place was packed, the smells of garlic and tomato heavy on the air. I piled in with my dads, grandparents, and siblings. Lottie was whiny and tired until she saw the inside of the pizza place, her favorite place in the *whole wide world* because they had pizza and paintings on the wall. The tables were covered with red and white checkered cloths, while fake candles flickered away in small glass jars placed on every tabletop. Our team was taking up about ten tables, the boosters and family the same. It was insanely loud. We all exchanged fist bumps as I passed, even Felix held up a hand. I tapped his lightly, then dropped down casually in a chair beside him, shrugging out of the letterman jacket I'd gotten last year. We all had them. Well, not all. The freshmen would get theirs at the end of the season. It made me proud to have one and show the campus that I was part of this team. Also, not going to fabricate, girls and guys really got into dating jocks. I'd had a girl I dated twice last year ask me for my jacket to wear. Yeah, no. That was only happening with someone incredibly special. Someone I was seeing exclusively.

"Nice penalty," Felix said as pitchers of soda were being plunked down on the tables.

I shot him a look and got one of those smirks that did strange things to me. I slowly scratched my chin with my middle finger making sure he saw it. The guys around us laughed, and Felix nodded, just once —blue eyes happy for once—and then, turned his attention to pouring himself some root beer. I'd made him smile. It was ridiculous how happy that made me.

---

HE WAS HERE, IN MY ROOM, AND WE WERE STUDYING, and jeez, I was totally cement boots-swimming-with-the-fishes sunk here.

"...thinking we should do this in an abstract set-up, right?"

I rolled my head to the left. Felix was lying beside me on the floor of my room, books and papers, white boards, and magic markers, scattered all around us while Post Malone's "I Like You (A Happier Song)" played out of my desktop speakers. I loved Post, and this collab with Doja Cat was fire. It also kind of described where my head was at as October settled on us with chilly nights, falling leaves, and a dance in two weeks. A dance for which I still had no date.

"Sure, that's cool." I held up my tablet, my heels resting on the wall under a poster of Dwight Schrute. Felix was in the same legs-up-the-wall pose, pillows lying under our asses to elevate our feet even more. According to my grandmother, this was a cool yoga move that helped ease leg stress, which we both had from a killer skate after school today. "We can work the pictures in at tilted angles. Make it more pop and less Ladies Journal of the Home, or whatever that magazine is."

He snickered, then tipped his tablet this way and that, the screen locked into place. "*Ladies Home Journal*, dork."

"How do you know that?"

"My housekeeper used to read it."

"Oh, cool. Is she nice? Your housekeeper?"

"Mm, yeah, Phoebe's nice. What do you think of adding more interviews?"

I rolled to my side, tucking my feet into a wonky sort of pretzel to accommodate my butt still resting on the wall. Well, one cheek was on the wall. It was a knotted-up pose that Grandma would, for sure, have a yoga pose name for, if she saw it.

"Yeah, that would be cool." I tucked my iPad into my chest to enjoy his profile. He smelled really good tonight. Like cherry vanilla soda. Short gold hair clung to his cheeks and eyelashes. I had to grip my tablet hard to keep my hands to myself. That hair on his lashes so needed to be gently brushed away from his eye...

"All right, cool. I like the idea of our articles not being so much about the boring-ass history of a building, but about the living, breathing people who work and go to Chesterford. That's so much more compelling."

He was so pretty to look at, especially when his bright eyes sparkled with creativity. His sight flicked from his tablet to me when I didn't reply. The moment his gaze met mine, that strange wobbly sensation erupted in my lower stomach. And it was not gas from Grandma's taco bake supreme, which we'd had for dinner. He moved to his side, his gaze never leaving mine, rolling closer until our noses were less than an inch apart. I stared into his eyes, loving all the different shades of sapphire, turquoise, and sunflower. Thick lashes swept down once, twice, and the third time, they rested on his cheek for a second before slowly rising.

I think I made the first move, but maybe we went for it at the same time? Hard to say when there was only a feather's distance between us. Whoever. Whatever. It didn't matter at all because his pillowy lips were now pressed to mine, and it was *everything*.

I'd kissed people before. I'd gone further than kissing a few times. I mean, I was going to be sixteen in five days. So yeah, the whole kissing thing shouldn't have hit me as it had. The kiss was tender and a little tentative. Amazingly hot, even with no tongues. My body was thrumming, blood heading south so fast I got a little dizzy.

Then, he drew back. I wet my lips to get more of the zing of his taste into my mouth. Felix stared at me as if I were some new species just discovered on the ocean floor.

"That was...I shouldn't have done that," I said weakly as he lay there gazing at me vacantly. "I know you're not into guys. I just…I'm sorry. Consent was totally not given."

"I moved in on you," he whispered, his voice so soft and slumberous that I had to strain to hear him. "I am into guys. Like exclusively, I think."

I blinked. Hard. Several times. If I had been in a sandstorm in the Sahara, I'd not have been blinking that steadily. Okay. Huh. Well, that explains… absolutely nothing. "Please, just…don't ask. Consent is totally given if you think you might like to do it again?"

He didn't have to ask twice. We kissed a dozen times, maybe two, all of them timid pecks that lingered only long enough for us to get into it, then we'd break apart.

"I'm not sure what to say," I breathlessly said after kiss fifteen or so. There were a ton of things that I wanted to say, to ask, but he'd asked me to let things ride, so I totally would. A thump outside my door right before someone knocked sent us slithering apart as if we were sidewinders.

"Hey guys. It's eleven o'clock. Time to break up the study fest. I'll take you home, Felix," Gramps said, gave us a wide smile, and then left, leaving my bedroom door open.

"Guess that's it," Felix said, his voice strained.

We gathered up his stuff in silence, neither of us sure of what the hell to say after the two dozen kisses. I walked him to the front door; Gramps gave me a nod, then led Felix out to his car, and they were gone, nothing but taillights in the dark.

It was crazy how the meeting of two sets of lips could change everything all at once.

## Chapter Fourteen

### Felix

"...AND THEY WENT STRAIGHT THROUGH ME, IF YOU know what I mean." Soren's gramp winked at me as he killed the engine, and I couldn't help smiling back at him. He was everything I think I wanted in grandparents, but the only ones I had were my mom's over in New York, who had never quite forgiven me for being the son of their daughter and her bad choice of husband. Sure, I saw them in the summer sometimes, and the odd Christmas, but it was more of an exchange of money for me being polite, rather than hugs and stories about the time Soren's gramp ate too many prunes.

"Thank you for taking me home," I said, and

smiled again, then opened the door to see him do the same.

"Only polite I say hello," he said.

I wasn't going to argue because I didn't know how to. I was still on a high from the kisses and the soft words shared with Soren. What did that mean? Were we seeing each other? Were we dating? Was it hormones? Would we be walking through school holding hands? Fuck... I couldn't even think about that now.

I headed around the back, Gramps in tow, and saw Rick first.

"Pleasure to meet you," Gramps began.

"That's not my dad," I began, and then wondered how to explain my relationship with Rick, but then it hit me exactly what to say. "He's like my best friend; he and his wife, Phoebe, they look after me."

Rick beamed at me, then extended one to Gramps.

"Soren's grandpa," Gramps said.

"Rick."

They didn't talk for long, shooting the breeze about the weather, and cars, and gardening, but Rick grasped my shoulder briefly as I went to pass him, and we exchanged smiles.

The kitchen door was open, and I dropped my bag

on the table and called my dad's name as loudly as I could without it actually reaching his study.

"He's probably still at a meeting," I explained to Gramps, who didn't argue at all, just copied Rick's gesture of squeezing my shoulder and offering me one final piece of advice as grandparents liked to do. Only it wasn't about me straightening my tie to not look scruffy, or to make sure I studied hard, this was more practical advice.

"Stay off the prunes," he said.

"Good advice," I said, and we chuckled and he left. Collision between dad and Soren's gramp avoided.

I grabbed a juice and snacks, and settled into the media room with my phone.

I needed answers, and maybe my phone could help, so I went into incognito mode in my browser—just in case—and began typing in questions.

*How do I be gay?* That returned way too many answers, and I already knew what I was—I only needed to frame my new life with that knowledge. I was gay, I was into boys, and mostly, I was into Soren.

Wait... I pulled up the browser and typed in a new question: *Can I just be gay for one person?* Several answers came up to that one, talking about the spectrum of sexuality, and I considered each one carefully. Was I attracted to Soren because my emotions were all over the place? Was it just me wanting to experiment? Or was this thing with Soren because I thought I hated him, and it turned out he wasn't a bad guy? Maybe, it was because his dad was Tennant Madsen-Rowe? That last thought made my chest tighten—Soren might well be related to Tennant, but that wasn't anything to do with it.

It went way further back than Soren.

Way back to James Dryden in math. He was a jock, a football player, cocky, self-assured, and I'd felt *things* when I looked at him with something akin to awe. He was perfect; he was my dream; he was everything I thought about until the day Soren started at Chesterford.

No, it wasn't just Soren.

But Soren had been the one to dominate all my thoughts since I'd first seen him.

Had lashing out at him been a self-defense mechanism for fighting my attraction to him? To the boy who'd been rescued from nothing, then handed everything on a plate? Did I think that now? Was I the worst person on the entire Earth, or just freaking confused? I clicked a few more links, opening a page on bisexuality. Was I bi if I liked some girl in her sweater even though I scoped out her sweater and not her boobs? I imagined kissing a girl, feeling all that softness against me, but it did nothing. I wanted strong hands, and the feel of a...

...I wanted Soren.

"Felix?" Dad interrupted my thoughts, and I hastily shut down all the incognito screens. There was no way I was ready to announce to my dad anything at all about Soren, or kissing, or the fact I thought I was gay.

"Everything okay?" He framed it as a question, still in that same doorway, still talking to me despite me not wanting to talk back because he was ruining my big epiphany and my rosy glow from kissing Soren.

"I was studying with Soren, his gramps dropped me back."

"Thank him for me."

I blinked at him. "Soren or his gramps?"

"His grandpa. For driving you. I was on a call trying to... nothing. I mean, I could have come and picked you up."

"I was okay."

"Can we talk?"

I carefully placed my phone to one side. "Yeah?"

He gestured at the couch, as if he needed my

permission to come in, and I nodded—Felix for *whatever*.

He took the opposite couch and reached over for the control, switching off the television. I tilted my chin because no doubt I'd messed up with something, and I should have known our truce was going to be broken. Maybe, he thought I'd talked to Mom, or left out a towel, or I was rude, or maybe, I was in the wrong place at the wrong time. It was probably because I'd tried to talk to Tyler—maybe, I'd looked at him the wrong way, or something, and he'd gone running to his mom. Great, now I was feeling stressed and wound up.

"What did I do now?" I asked with exaggerated patience.

"Nothing. You didn't do anything. Look…" He stopped, then shuffled forward so he was on the very edge of the couch. "We have a decision to make, together, the two of us. The reason I was in a meeting… I was talking to my lawyer. I've tried really hard to fight this Felix, but your mom is shutting down the Harrisburg office. She's selling this house from under me, and I'd like us to move to—"

"Hang on. I know how much you're worth Dad, I follow the stocks every day."

"On paper. Everything I have is tied up in the

company. We had a pre-nup when I was so young I never even knew what I was signing, and it didn't matter because I loved your mom then. I loved her." He scrubbed at his eyes.

"I know you did," I murmured because it seemed like the right thing to say.

"This is your mom's house; any money I have is your mom's money. Not mine."

"She'll give it to me, and you can stay," I said with confidence. My mom might have slowly, but surely, removed herself from my life, but she was still my mom.

He stared at the floor, and his shoulders drooped. "She's listed it. Today."

"Then stop her." I don't know why I was even arguing because it wasn't as if I loved this house—I hated it. But this was where Phoebe and Rick were, and if we moved, would I lose them, would it just be me on my own? Or with Dad? Everything abruptly piled onto me, the kisses forgotten, my momentary peace shattered. I pressed a hand to my heart as it raced and adrenaline flowed through me like lava, burning and hissing and destroying every shred of rational thinking.

Was dad preparing me for something? Was he leaving? Would I be completely alone?

"We need to look for somewhere else—"

"You do!" I snapped. "You find something else for you, because I'm not losing Phoebe and Rick—I'll live with them!"

His face twisted, and I thought he was going to cry. "You'll never lose Phoebe and Rick. I'll ask them to come with us, wherever we go. I know you think I don't care; I know you don't trust me, and hell, I know your mom and I are to blame, but Felix, I want us to start again because you're my son."

"On paper," I echoed his earlier words, and he winced as if I'd actually punched him. Maybe, right about now, I could do with hitting something because I wanted my golden glow back. "I deserve parents who actually give a damn... but you know what? Never mind. I'm done with all of that. You're getting a divorce, so I get to choose where I live, end of."

"I thought we could stay around here, and you'd live with me so you can stay at Chesterford?" I couldn't handle all this crying and emotion. "But son, if you want to be with your mom, I won't fight it."

What? Why wouldn't he fight it? Didn't he want me? I was his son! Fuck them both. If neither of them wanted me, then I'd find somewhere else, live with a friend... I didn't have any real friends... I had Soren.

My head was a mess.

"I hate you for saying that! I'm leaving. I don't know where, but I'm finished with all of this."

"Son, I didn't mean I wanted you to leave—"

"I hate you, and I hate Mom." I stood up, even as my dad's face crumpled. "Did you hear me? I hate you!" Yeah, I wanted to hurt him, because hurting him was real and honest and payback for all the times I'd locked myself in here to escape my parents' fighting, with him backing down every single time. It left me cold.

And hurting people was what I'd learned to be good at.

Then, I realized he was stumbling back, and back, until he landed on the couch, his hand on his chest, and he was doubling over in pain. "What's wrong? What are you doing?"

He looked up at me, his eyes unfocused, his breathing harsh. "911."

THE JOURNEY TO THE HOSPITAL WAS A BLUR. THE paramedics arrived within ten minutes, but it seemed like an hour when all I could do was hold my dad's hand and pray I hadn't just killed him with the blades of hate I'd thrown at him. Then, it was a full day before they told me what had happened, with no sign of my mom, even though I'd called and left her a message. Even if she didn't come here for Dad, even if she hated him as much as I'd said I did, surely she'd be here for her son. Right? I spent way too long waiting in the chair by Dad's bed. Waiting for a diagnosis, for him to come back from surgery after he'd had a pacemaker fitted, to know he'd be okay.

Waiting for Mom.

I left five messages before I even got an answer. For the longest time, I stared at it as if the letters might rearrange themselves and tell me that she loved me, and she'd be here for me. Nothing changed—the message stayed the same.

*It's not good for my mental health to be there right now.*

There wasn't even a kiss. Not that we were a demonstrative family, but still, one solitary $X$ would have been enough for me to think she was at least considering her son in all of this.

"Hey," Phoebe said from the door. She and Rick had been a constant. She'd run to the house when I'd called her to say that Dad had fallen. "We're going to get some lunch, what can I get you?"

I pulled my legs up on the chair and wrapped my

arms around my knees. "I'm okay." I felt sick and shocked, and I wasn't okay at all.

"I'll bring you something," she murmured, but I wasn't even looking at her. I was staring at Dad, still but breathing, his eyes not opening yet. I think she left, but it was another woman's voice saying hello that pulled me from my focus, and for a moment, hope lifted my heart. But it wasn't Mom, it was Lilly Corrigan, and hovering behind her, Tyler. Both of them seemed at a loss for what to do, and after that brief hello from her, it seemed that was all she could manage.

I guess it was up to me to ask them in, but I took a moment to get my first real glance at Tyler's mom— one that didn't involve me acting out because I thought she was wedging herself between Mom and Dad. She was shorter than Tyler, a slight woman with long dark hair, but I could see where Tyler got his wide eyes from, and his bone structure. I could understand what Dad might see in her, but the thought of that, against the fact my dad was in a freaking hospital bed, was just too much to come to terms with.

"Hi," Tyler added, neither of them making a move to come in. I know they weren't officially allowed into the room unless they were family, but they were here now, so what were they waiting for? An engraved invitation maybe? Fuck, even now I couldn't switch off that snarky nasty side of my brain. *I'm broken.* I rested my chin on my knees, and stared at them, and finally, Tyler broke the impasse, taking a breath before he started.

"We just wanted to say hi, and that we're sorry your dad is in here, and that if you need anything from school, I can bring it to you, and if you need Mom to do anything, just ask," he said in one run-on sentence, then glanced at his mom who was suspiciously red-eyed.

I didn't have words. I didn't have *anything*. I was numb, but somehow, his earnest promise of help, and the fact that they'd even shown up, was what I needed.

"Thank you," I offered in a small voice, grateful when Phoebe and Rick appeared, and I could sit quiet and small as they talked about things that I didn't even tune in to.

"Can I get you anything?" Tyler startled me, and I realized he was standing in front of me. I shook my head, and he didn't push me, and for that, I was grateful.

When he and his mom left, and Phoebe and Rick went out to fetch things from home—just for something to do—it was just me and Dad again. I scooted the chair closer to the bed and took his hand, willing him to move his fingers and lace them together with mine. A nurse came in to take his vitals and asked me if I was okay. I bobbed my head, my thoughts all about Dad, and us going home.

All I could think was that I'd told him I hated him, and if he died...

I buried my head in the covers of his bed and tried to calm my frantic breathing, tightening my hold on Dad's hand, and willing him to be okay.

*Please.*

# Chapter Fifteen

## Soren

WHEN THURSDAY ENGLISH CLASS STARTED AND there was still no Felix, I began to worry. I mean a couple days off due to a cold or something was normal, but more than that? I'd tried messaging him about the project—not about the kissing because I didn't want that on my phone, at least not yet. But was he avoiding me because of the kissing?

Nearly a week of him not being at school, and no texts about this dumb magazine, was something else. Was I pissed that I'd had to do the outline by myself in a rush? Yes. Not that I minded the work… okay, I totally did because I had enough of my own to do, and Felix not pulling his weight was shitty. Also, it kept me from streaming, which was something I loved doing to reduce stress. Stress caused by my English project partner bagging on school and hockey. So yeah, I was mad because we were now falling behind on this stupid assignment. And Felix, aka Richie Rich, was probably off on a fall retreat in St. Barthélemy, soaking up the sun, getting a tan, and making passes at the pretty French West Indies girls. Why would he ghost me after we kissed? Did he regret those kisses now?

I was here working my ass off on this—

"Hey," I heard behind me. I glanced over my shoulder after shoving my chem book into my locker to find Tyler leaning on the bank of blue lockers to my left, right next to a jack-o-lantern poster put up for Halloween. "You going to hockey practice after school?"

"Yeah." I pulled out the books I'd need for homework, then shut my locker to face him.

"Will you do me a favor?" He looked stressed, tight lines around his mouth as students escaped from the last class of the day to catch buses or meet their rides home.

"Sure." I hefted my backpack up one arm, then reached back to thread my left arm through the dangling strap.

"Will you tell Coach that I won't be there tonight because I'm going with my mom to visit Jim in the hospital?"

"Oh, yeah, will do." I had no clue who Jim was, but if he was in the hospital, then that seemed serious. "Just make sure you get a note from your mom for next Monday's practice or Coach will bench you. Felix is going to be riding the lumber for sure for missing two skates this week."

Mr. Iglesias stalked up, his gaze flicking to Tyler and me talking. "I'm sure you gentlemen have something better to do than loiter in the halls and slow the flow of student traffic," he sniped before hurrying on to say the same thing to a group of girls chatting outside a bathroom. I gave his lanky back a glower as he made the rounds being Super Hall Monitor.

"Nah, he's gotten an extended medical leave excuse because of Jim's heart attack."

That pulled me back from shooting dark looks at the crabby American History teacher nudging us all to stop being social in school. Like, wasn't the point of school to be social? Adults made no sense.

"Who's Jim?" I asked, my aggravation melting away to be replaced by concern.

"Felix's dad," Tyler replied, a wild shank of hair

dangling into his eye. "He's been sick for like a week now."

"Oh shit," I whispered, feeling really crappy now. I'd bitched long and hard for days about Felix skipping out on his work. Damn. I was a jerk. "Why didn't he reach out to me? Why didn't *you* tell me?"

Tyler was confused, "I didn't think that you would want to know about Felix?"

"We have a project, and he has my number..." I defended.

Tyler shrugged. "Yeah well, he seems kind of out of it. He's been getting his homework assignments online so he's staying up on his class work. Coach said he could put him on the injured list if he has to stay out longer, but I figure he'll be back next week, probably. They're hiring a nurse to stay with Jim until he's back on his feet, so he won't need Felix around to help."

"Wow," I said again because that was all I could think of to say. "Man, that sucks. Thanks for telling me."

"No problem. Thanks for letting Coach know. My phone is dead, and I have to meet Mom out front like ten minutes ago. Thank god the trip to Harrisburg Medical Center is a fast one, or she'd be birthing a bison." We bumped fists, and Tyler took off like a hare, moving gracefully through the crowds of kids as I stood there staring at a poster about the Halloween dance at the end of October. I'd been wondering who I would ask to go with me. Now, that seemed a little inconsequential in light of the news about Felix's dad.

My head hurt. What would I do if Jared or Ten were deathly sick? Milo and I had only been their legal sons for a short while, just a couple of years, but I loved both of them. If either one were to get seriously ill or hurt in a game, I'd…well, I'd say the hell with everything and be at their sides, exactly like Felix had done. I stared at the smiling jack-o-lantern for the longest time, long enough for Mr. Iglesias to come back around and prod me to get moving.

For some strange reason, I decided to skip going for ramen after practice to go visit Felix. I sent Ten a quick text telling him to skip picking me up after our drills today. I'd take the bus to the hospital, then home. Mass transit didn't faze me at all. I'd grown up using it or walking. Milo and I didn't have a fancy car with a loving parent out front of our schools until Ten and Jared had taken us into their home. When Ten asked if I was okay, I explained. He hit me back saying that it was fine, he would send flowers to Jim's room, and to wish Felix and his family our best.

Focusing on hockey was hard. My head kept

pulling me into deep, dark scenarios about my own fathers. Jared had a heart condition of some sort. Ten had suffered a head injury in a game years ago, and the effects of that brain bleed still lingered with crippling headaches on occasion. So what if one of them got sick? What if both died? They flew all over the place during the season, which was kicking off in a few weeks. Training camp was already rolling for the Railers. What would the three of us do, if they were in a plane that crashed over the Rockies? Who would take care of us? Would Milo and I be back on the streets? Who would get Lottie? Could I keep her? I loved her like my own sister. Would we live with Grandma and Grandpa? Or with Uncle Brady or Uncle Jamie? Would they split us up and make us live in separate states? No way was that happening.

No one was taking Milo or Lottie from me.

I'd fucking die on that hill.

My head was a mess. Coach was not impressed with my performance during our drills and told me to get my brain in the game. I *was* trying, honestly. The bus ride to the huge medical center sitting on the banks of the Susquehanna River did little to flush the concerns for my parents away. Padding through the main doors, I paused to grab a mask, then entered the massive building. I stopped at the main desk to get directions to

CICU with firm information that I'd not be allowed in to see the patient if I wasn't a family member. Which was fine. I made a fast stop at the gift shop and picked up a bouquet of flowers for Jim and a stuffed pelican for Felix. I had no clue what it was about the dorky bird with the bill filled with tiny candies from a local chocolate factory, but something about it spoke to me.

Exiting on the fourth floor, I came face-to-face with a nurse's station. When I enquired about James Maxwell-Sinclair I was told he was in stable condition, and that was all I got from the dark-haired woman in white.

"I'll tell the family you're here. You can wait in one of our lounges."

"Cool, I'll be over there." I jerked a thumb at a sunny lounge with gray and blue loveseats. She nodded and returned to her paperwork. I ambled into the room, dropped my backpack on a gray couch, and hit up the vending machines along the far wall. With a grape soda and a bag of chips, I settled in with my phone. The wait wasn't too long. I glanced up to see Felix in the doorway, staring at me as if I were an alien pod spore floating in the sunny rays pouring through the double-pane windows with the other motes.

"The nurse said you were here," Felix said, his bright blue eyes dull from worry and lack of sleep. He had dark rings under those usually snapping sapphire eyes. "What the hell are you doing here?"

"I just found out about your dad." I stood trying my best to ignore the sour cream and onion chip crumbs falling from my shirt to the floor. Felix picked them up, of course. I dusted my belly off. He zoned in on that motion, too, then grew even angrier-looking. "My dads are sending flowers."

"Yeah, we just got them." He remained in the doorway, leery, as if he were about to step into a lion's den. "They are nice."

"Good. Well, I brought these up for him." I scooped up the flowers and held the bouquet out to him. "And this is for you." I extended the pelican out to him, too. He eyed the little stuffed bird as if it were packed full of C-4. "He reminded me of you for some reason."

"Thanks?" He finally stepped into the lounge to take the flowers and the pelican.

"Yeah, I think his big bill full of food made me think of you when we were at the ramen place and your cheeks were packed full of noodles." He made a sour face, but it lacked his usual quality snark.

"Anyway, I am sorry about your dad. Is he okay? Tyler said they put a pacemaker in?"

"Yeah, no, he's okay." He walked to the window to gaze down at the river slowly flowing past, the flowers and pelican clasped to his chest. "It's a pretty simple procedure now. They've got him stable so he can go home tomorrow."

I padded over to stand at his side, my sight on the river as well. "That's great."

"Yeah." He sighed, his hold on the flowers and pelican tightening. The stems on the daisies were taking a throttling, and the poor bird was horking up his chocolate kisses. "It's been…he almost died in front of me."

I had no fucking clue what to say to that, so I kept my mouth shut and reached over to rub his bicep. His arm was firm under the wrinkled gray Railers tee. His muscle flexed at the touch, then, imperceptibly, began to relax as his jaw began to wobble.

"Felix?"

He shuddered. "We were fighting; he was trying to be cool, you know?"

I nodded because, yeah, I did know. Dads tried to be cool. Sometimes it worked, and sometimes, like when Jared had sung and twerked to a Meghan Thee Stallion song at Milo's birthday party over the summer, it failed epically. I saw the tsunami of emotions roaring over Felix and was helpless to do anything but rub his arm harder when the crush of the last few days barreled into him.

"I was being a jerk," he gasped, the pelican losing all his treats, the flowers falling to the side, their stems smashed. "I was yelling at him. I… I told him that I hated him."

The tears fell then, despite his best efforts to keep them at bay. They ran down his scruffy cheeks, wetting the patchy golden whiskers.

"You didn't mean it," I said, easing my arm around his shoulders.

The sobs hit him hard. I tugged him into my chest, the sideways hug awkward, but enough that he could at least rest his face on my shoulder. Someone walked past the open door, rubber-soled shoes squeaking on the freshly mopped tile floor.

"He could have died, and those would have been my last words to him. How fucked up is that?" He gasped.

A page for a doctor flowed through the speakers, replacing the piped-in 70s soft rock for a moment. I held him close, unable to form words that would help him with the guilt. I knew that burden. I'd said some pretty shitty things to Ten and Jared when we'd first met them and were feeling each other out. I'd trusted no one over the age of thirty, and for good reason, for all the adults I'd ever dealt with had let me and Milo down. Of course, I wished I could take back those terrible things now, but words spoken in anger can never be erased.

"We all say shit when we're angry or scared," I finally managed to say, hoping it didn't sound stupid and trite. "He knows you love him."

He snuffled in a really undignified way. A sound that was far beneath anything Felix Maxwell-Sinclair would normally make. His head left my shoulder, and he stared at me with red-rimmed eyes filled with such pain it made my gut cramp.

"I do," he whispered thickly, his eyelashes clumpy with tears. "I just hate all the fighting. You know, Mom isn't even here."

"She went out to get something?"

"She never even arrived."

That sounded bad. I nodded as if I knew what fighting he was talking about. Truthfully, I had no idea what was going on in his house. He wasn't exactly the most open guy in the world, but if I had to guess, he probably meant his parents.

"It sucks when parents fight," I chanced and got a confused, tearful look. "Ten and Jared do on occasion, little stuff mostly, like one not putting the cap back on the toothpaste or the other not picking up socks. Shit like that. Milo and I lived with a couple when we were in the system who fought constantly. Loud, nasty fights. Things would get thrown. Walls would be punched. Milo and I would hide in our bedroom closet, him in my arms, until the house was quiet, then we'd sneak out and go to bed. Milo slept with me for the entire two years we were with them, and even now, if Ten and Jared get loud, he comes to find me."

Felix bent his head, swiped at his face with the back of the hand holding the crumpled bouquet, and hit me in the nose with a wilted tulip. That, for some reason, made him laugh. Like out loud, as if the funniest comedian in the world had just delivered the best joke ever. He laughed so hard I had to hold him up. Talk about a rollercoaster of emotions.

We ended up back on the couch, him panting, me snickering at his belly laughs. I had never heard him laugh before. He had a strong laugh. He should really do it more; it made his face bright and sunny.

"I think I'm losing my shit," he coughed out as he slowly caught his breath.

"It's been a week," I tossed out for him, and he nodded vigorously. "Want a soda?"

"Yeah please, thanks." He sat on the couch, his knees rubbery, and placed the flowers on the glass table beside a pile of magazines. The pelican, he held onto, and that made me feel good inside. I bought him a cold can of Coke and passed it to him before making a sweep to pick up the spilled silver candies from the floor. When I sat down, I peeled one and offered it to him.

"Milo says that the best thing for crying is chocolate," I said as I dropped the tiny drop of delectableness into Felix's shaky palm.

"He's wise beyond his years," he replied, then popped the candy into his mouth. We sat in silence for a few, letting him drink some soda and eat some chocolate. "Thanks for coming by. You're the only person from school, other than Tyler, who's made the effort, and he was here with his mom for my dad, not for me."

"Well, to be fair, no one apart from Tyler knew." I flicked a silver ball into the trash. "Swish."

"Miles and Jonah know," he said in a small voice. "I texted them."

"Oh." I tried not to be hurt that he hadn't called or texted me, particularly after those kisses and thinking that, maybe, we had the start of something. Then, I pushed that down—now wasn't the time for me to feel hurt, now was the time for me to be here for Felix. I handed him another candy. "Miles and Jonah are assholes, you know that, right? Well Miles is anyway; Jonah is just… Jonah."

He let out a weary breath. "Yeah, I know. I think I am, too."

"Yeah, you totally are." I nudged him in the side and passed him a chocolate drop.

"Takes one to know one," he replied with a shaky smile, and the world felt a little sunnier. Or maybe, it was just me overdosing on the tingles that his thigh next to mine and his snarky little smirk created.

Yeah, probably the latter.

Totally the latter.

## Chapter Sixteen

### Felix

THE FIRST DAY BACK AT SCHOOL WAS AN EYE-OPENER. There was no sign of Miles or Jonah waiting in their normal spot under the tree by the drop-off zone, but that might be because they hadn't known I was coming back. I mean, I'd messaged them last night, but they'd never answered, so I assumed they didn't see the message.

Or they didn't want to know, which was more likely.

In their place, a little further down, was Soren, his foot against the wall behind him as he stared up at the blue sky. I hadn't told *him* I was coming back today, and the very thought that he was waiting here for me was ludicrous. He had to be waiting for Tyler, or Courtney, or one of the others in his group of friends, so I tilted my chin and pulled my invisible cloak of he-can't-see-me close around me, then sauntered past and tried, desperately, not to think of sugar-sweet kisses and the way he stared at me when our lips met, or the way that I felt so confused about everything.

"Hey," he called as he jogged over from his spot to fall in at my side, then knocked elbows with me.

"Hey," I answered and side-eyed him. "What's up?" I couldn't believe he'd been waiting for *me* to arrive this morning. He probably wanted to talk about the project because we had to be behind now, and I'd ignored all his texts. I'd ignored them because, every time I saw his name, I felt confused and horny and messed up and weird, and it wasn't a good feeling. Well, it *was* a good feeling—the horny part anyway.

"It's always hard coming into school after time off," Soren said as we joined the short line for the scanners, which were stainless steel and incongruous against the old stone of the main building. "Thought you might like company is all."

He faced me, and his hand brushed mine, and for a brief, shining moment, I thought maybe we would hold hands, or that he'd lean in and kiss me, but he stepped back out of reach. I got the message—no

PDA and no admission of the accident that had been our lips touching. Maybe the kissing had been nothing other than messing about, and we certainly weren't acknowledging in public that it had happened.

"I don't need company." My usual defense mechanism had slipped effortlessly into place. I couldn't *let* myself need anything because then I could never be disappointed. Simple.

"Tough. You've got it," Soren said, in that infuriating tone of his that meant he didn't care what I thought.

We passed through the scanners, then took a right toward the auditorium, and just before we reached our lockers, he tugged me to the left, down the corridor and another turn, and into a bathroom. I didn't even know this bathroom existed, then I saw it was marked *visitors,* so it clearly wasn't for students. I could have balked at being dragged in there, but Soren was digging his heels in, and the part of me that recalled the kissing wanted to hear what he had to say, if only to rip the Band-Aid off because this was the moment he told me what we'd done was stupid, and he wasn't into me, and that each of the kisses were a lie. Hashtag inevitable.

He pushed the door shut, and I got my first look inside a visitor's bathroom. There were soft towels, one cubicle, and the biggest mirror I'd seen in the school. There were three jars of hand cream—not pump dispensers, jars—and matching soaps in a dish, and the whole place smelled so good, like lavender or something.

"No one comes in here," Soren said and picked up a soap to toss it into the air.

"Unless they're visitors," I deadpanned.

He shrugged. "Then we tell them we're sorry and make a run for it. What can they do?"

"The visitors?"

"Them and the school?"

"I don't know." What were we even discussing?

"First offense," Soren announced and leaned back on the unit where there were dual sinks with fancy taps. From the look of the walls, this must be part of one of the front extensions, the ones where they needed to hide everything behind the brick façade that was dark green with ivy. "It's safe in here," he added.

"Safe from what?"

"Questions, people beating on other people, that kind of thing." He held my gaze. "Tyler showed it to me."

I swear, I could feel the heat burning me from inside—I was probably scarlet with the shame of everything. He was talking about *me*, about the things

*I'd* done to Tyler, and this was what? A reckoning? The kisses lulled me into thinking he was a good guy, and now, he was going to punch me and leave me in the bathroom. I think I took a step back, but he grasped my hand and tugged me toward him.

"Don't look like that," he whispered.

"What?"

"Scared. It was just kissing. It doesn't have to mean anything."

Disappointment flooded me and settled in my chest, heavy as a rock. "Oh. Okay," I attempted to tug my hand free, but he held it.

"Anything bad I mean, because it could mean something good, y'know," he said, and my heart filled with stupid hope. "I don't have all the words you might need to hear. I don't have the fancy education and the manners. I'm just me, the guy who looks out for his little brother, the one who wants to get through school and get out the other side without failing. I just know…"

He placed a finger under my chin to lift my face, and I realized, somehow, I'd stopped looking at him. Then, he slipped his hand up to cradle my cheek, and it was the softest of touches, but it felt so solid, as if he could hold me there and protect me.

Protect me? From what? Parents? Moving to a new house? School? Hockey?

Or maybe, he could protect me from myself.

I pressed my cheek against his hand, lost in the warmth of his dark eyes, uncaring that we were in school, that we were in a bathroom we weren't allowed into, and that we were going to be late to class.

"Felix?" he leaned toward me.

I reached up and covered his hand with mine, then we slowly drifted into another kiss, a gentle press of lips that was the same as what we'd shared in his room. What was I doing? Was my kissing okay? I'd never kissed an actual boy before Soren, but I'd practiced on my hand. Was that gross? Was I gross? How would he even…

The tip of his tongue traced my lips, poked at the seam of them, and with a sigh I opened my mouth a little so he could dart inside and taste me—so I could taste him. I was so scared. What if I did this wrong, what if everything I'd read about gentle and searching should have read more like thrusting and poking, and I was messing it all up? His other hand came up to cradle me completely, and I moaned low into the kiss, a begging breathy sound he caught in the kiss. I heard him chuckle, but it was low and easy, and then, he tilted my head and pulled back.

"Is this okay?" he asked.

"Yes. But…"

"But what?"

I was mortified. "Am I doing this right?"

"I want to kiss you again. Can I?"

This was *him* asking *me* for permission, and right now, I wanted it all. Kissing Soren meant I didn't have to think about anything outside this small room, kissing him was hot and emotional, and all of it caught in my throat as I nodded.

With a smile on his lips, he kissed me again, and this time around, I fell into everything with eagerness, and for the first time, my tongue met his—tangling lazy and slow, tasting, and touching—and I was so hard, and so lost in the absolute perfection of this moment. Since that day in the hospital when I'd cried all over him, it seemed as if all my feelings were so close to the surface that I worried they'd spill out again, but this kiss was everything, and I didn't care about tears pricking my eyes, or that I was so turned on I could come in my freaking pants right here and now. He tugged me a little closer and deepened the kiss, and I was lost.

We only parted when the first bell sounded.

"Are you coming out with us after practice?" he asked softly, as he straightened the strap of my backpack on my shoulder.

"Will the others want me to?"

"Sure, they will." He could be lying, but I didn't care as he pressed one last kiss to my lips, and sue me if I chased for more even though I knew we had to leave. I might get some leeway with it being the first day back, but Soren wouldn't get dispensation at all. He spent a while rearranging his clothes to cover being as turned on as I was, tugging down his jacket, before he grinned at me. "Uh oh."

I hid my erection as best I could, and then, he ushered me out, with him close behind, and this time, when our hands touched, he briefly laced our fingers and squeezed. First class was chem, and I'd missed even more of what was going on in this higher-level class, but buoyed by the kisses, I went into the class with a smile, knowing I could handle anything today. Next class, I was with Soren, and if that didn't make me smile, nothing could.

Apart from Miles, who scowled at me in the hallway, stared at me in math, and then, tracked me down at first break as I rummaged in my locker to find my English notes. Miles gripped my jacket, dragged me into the nearest boy's bathroom, which stank and was a lot less fancy than the one I'd been in this morning. He kicked open each of the four doors, then sent a frosh running with a glare when they dared to step inside. I didn't like the look of fear on the kid's face. Jeez, wasn't that something—I'd never cared before.

"What's up?" I asked Miles, and yelped when he shoved me back against the sink and held me there, his grip on my arms tight.

"Turns out your dad isn't all that!" He shouted right in my face, pushing me harder, the counter digging into my thigh. "Turns out he's nothing now my mom has been let go, and I don't have to pretend to want to be around you anymore."

"Miles—"

"The times you made me feel like I was two inches tall, like just because my mom works for your dad that you have something over me, and now, he's let her go, and we're fucked, and the only good I can get out of all of it, is that I get to leave you bleeding in a bathroom."

Very genuine fear bloomed inside me. Miles was a big guy, a linebacker, built and way taller than me, and even now, he was lifting me off my feet.

"I'm sorry, I didn't know about your mom—"

He shook me like a ragdoll, then shoved me away

so hard that I stumbled and went to my knees, hitting my head on the corner of the counter. I didn't even fight to get up—I deserved whatever was coming to me because the fear and pain was payback for how I'd been with Tyler, and how I'd pretended to be better than everyone here.

"I'm sorry," I said again, waiting for the kick, or the punch, but there was nothing, and then, I heard the door slam, and when I looked up, Miles was gone. I used the counter to stand up, pressing at the side of my head where it had connected with the tile, and thankfully, my hair covered the obvious bump. I straightened my tie and my jacket, and swallowed when I saw a very small and stupid kid staring back at me.

Was this how Tyler felt? Scared, sad? No wonder he hated me. I hated me.

I headed out, head down, and peered through every window I could find, knowing Tyler had to be in sciences somewhere, compelled to find him as soon as I could. I saw him in the last room on the left, bent over a notebook, scribbling furiously. Taking a deep breath, I knocked on the door and poked my head in. Mrs. James, head of Physics turned with a frown, but that frown softened when she saw me, and I was sure there was probably some bulletin out there telling teachers it was my first day back.

"Yes, Felix?" she asked after a moment.

"I need Tyler," I said, and pointed at him in case there was any confusion. "I mean, the principal asked for Tyler."

Tyler's eyes widened, and he scooped his notes into his bag and was at my side in an instant, his expression fearful. Shit, I never meant to worry him. We closed the classroom door, and he was asking questions straight away.

"Is it Mom? No! Is he back—"

"I'm sorry," I interjected.

He blinked at me. "What? Is it my mom?"

"No. Your mom is fine... no it's me. I'm so fucking sorry for what I did to you, the way I scared you. I'm sorry."

We were right in the middle of the corridor, and he stared back at me as if I had horns.

"You... I was in class... and you..." He thumped me in the chest. "You scared me, asshole," he muttered.

"Sorry."

Tyler examined me closely. "Wait." He brushed his pale pink bangs from his forehead and put his hands on his hips.

"Wait what?" I asked with caution.

"So, you're sorry you scared me by dragging me out of class to tell me you're sorry you scared me before."

I digested the words. "Pretty much, yeah."

He rolled his eyes at me, then thumbed at the room behind him. "Can I go back in now?"

"Wait," I said as he began to turn. "What was that about your mom?"

He shook his head, mute, and then, sighed. "Nothing."

I wanted to push him to tell me more, but he wasn't giving me a thing, and now, I felt stupidly awkward. "I'm sorry, yeah?"

He narrowed his eyes, but then, he smiled at me, and it reached his kohl-smudged eyes. "Sure."

Suddenly, it was vital I knew everything in black and white. I didn't expect him to forgive me, but I wanted to at least begin working things out with him —get him to trust me. "So, we're cool?"

He shrugged. "We might be cool, one day."

I deserved that. "I am sorry."

He nodded, "I know." Then, he pressed a hand to my arm. "We all do what we need to survive school," he murmured. "It's all good."

He went back into the classroom, and I stood

there for a few moments until a hand fell on my shoulder.

"What are you doing in the hallway?" the voice asked—Mr. Iglesias—and I pasted the most pathetic look on my face and turned to face him.

"Emotions," I murmured.

He backed away immediately, as if he expected me to cry, when all I wanted to do was grin. "Okay. Of course," he said. "Do you need to see someone?"

I blinked up at him. "I just need you to take me to my next class, and y'know…" I shrugged, "explain to the teacher."

"Of course," he said and tried for a smile of support.

It truly looked like he had gas.

## Chapter Seventeen

### Soren

I REALLY WASN'T SURE LIFE COULD BE MUCH BETTER.

Truth. The only snag in my existence right now was the fact that Felix and I were hiding our relationship. Sneaking around sucked, not going to lie. What we would do when our magazine project was completed, and we no longer had the studying excuse to fall back on, worried me. I didn't want to press him to come out. Totally not my place. We all had to do that in our own time, but I kept seeing those posters for the Halloween dance on seemingly every wall in Chesterford Academy.

Being a greedy POS, I wanted to ask Felix to go with me. I couldn't even seem to entertain the idea of asking someone else, not now that I knew how good he tasted, how fine he felt in my arms, how well we jibed. The entire student body paled in comparison.

We'd just had a hurried rendezvous in the biology lab not thirty minutes ago. You'd think the smell of formaldehyde would curb our lust, but nope. We were still crazy horny for kissing each other, even if there were containers of dead frogs watching us.

Which was why I was still entertaining the idea of going stag a few days before the dance. Also, it was why I was hiding in the library with my PennDOT Driver's Manual. A few girls had been eyeballing me at lunch. Guess the pickings were getting slim, and they were desperate. I'd noted the long looks and run to the darkest corner of the library to study.

I'd been hitting this manual hard since my birthday and the small family gathering we'd had the last time the dads were home. I'd not wanted much. Seemed a waste of cash to dump tons of green on a party for me. Milo and Lottie? Sure, they were kids. I wasn't. Not anymore. A birthday was simply another day. That was something I'd learned from being in the system. I'd lived through at least three birthdays that had gotten no recognition. Ten and Jared had balked at first, but they'd given in finally, so I suspected they were planning something big for this weekend. What,

I didn't know, but they'd been acting awfully cagey the past few days.

Someone tapped me on my shoulder. I let my head fall back to find Courtney standing behind me looking cute as hell in her little bubble gum-pink sweater. Her hair was pulled into a dozen quirky ponytails.

"Hey," I replied as she dropped into a chair beside me, her backpack thudding to the table. "Did you know that driving too fast for conditions is the number one reason why sixteen- and seventeen-year olds are involved in crashes? Says so right here." I tapped the screen of my tablet. "My dads would kill me if I wrecked one of their cars or got tapped for speeding."

"They're not the only ones who want to kill you," she sniped. I blinked in shock, lowering my tablet, the PDF of Pennsylvania driver laws coming to rest on my knees. "What the hell is going on with you and Felix?"

Oh. Shit. "Nothing," I lied, the dishonesty tasting bitter AF.

"Do *not* lie to me," she snapped, then got a shush from the kids sitting a few tables over. "I saw you two entering Mrs. Montgomery's lab when I was coming out of my ecology class. You were holding hands and whispering when you ducked into that room."

*Shit. Shit. Shit.* I stared up at the prune-faced woman in the painting above the fireplace. She seemed even grumpier.

"I can explain," I whispered, giving the other kids a worried look. All it would take would be one whispered comment to out Felix. I didn't want that on my conscience.

"I hope so because when I peeked through the window on the door you two were trying to eat each other's faces." She threw her arms over her chest, her expression thunderous. "Why are you making out with him?!"

"Would you *please* keep your voice down?" I spat, then rose. "Come with me." I shoved my tablet into my backpack, then stalked out of the library, Courtney stomping along in my wake. It was amazing how much noise her tiny feet made in those teensy black leather patents. We exploded out the doors into a chilly fall day. Gray clouds hung low in the sky, dead leaves danced down sidewalks, and the air had that autumnal tang to it.

I walked fast, my mind whirling, until we reached the statue of some old dude who had been one of the school's biggest donors in the late forties. Silas something. Not important ATM.

Courtney planted her feet by the statue's base. "Well?"

"Okay, so it's like this." I scanned the campus. Students were milling around in windbreakers, hoodies and jackets tightly zipped, hoods up. I tried to pick my words carefully because this was important. "We're kind of hanging out."

Her one eyebrow quirked. "You two looked like more than hang-out buddies. You two look like you're way more than that. Are you two hooking up?"

"What? No, we're not." That was true. We'd not gotten past some heavy kissing and rubbing. Nothing more than that. Felix wasn't ready, and I was down with that. I'd never done it either, so I was happy to wait. I wanted it to be special for us. "We're not hooking up at all. We're just…" And here I floundered.

"Felix is a jerk. A total asshole jerk homophobe. You hated him two months ago, and now, you and he are all over each other? What did I miss?" She was not backing down, and I didn't blame her. "I'm supposed to be your best friend!" Her eyes got dewy.

Shit. "Court, honestly, if I could've told you, I would have." I sucked in a long breath, held it as a dozen dried out oak leaves swirled past my sneakers, then let it out. "Okay, so there are things that you don't know."

"No shit!" She swiped at a tear that was tracking down her cheek. Ugh, I was a terrible person.

"Felix isn't out yet." It kind of tumbled out of me. I didn't know what else to say or do. Her eyes rounded. "It's all confusing for him, but he is into guys."

"Yeah, that was pretty obvious by the way he was trying to swallow your face." Some of the anger on her face softened. I parked my ass on Silas's plinth as she began to try to parse. "Okay." She sat beside me, our backsides resting on the cold cement, feet out to support us, hands now tucked under armpits as the wind was growing rawer by the minute. "So, I need the whole story." I opened my mouth. She held up a hand. "Nope, don't say it. I know this is a secret since he's not out. You know nothing gets out of me." I did know that. Some of the things we had shared since I arrived here would have been social death blows if we had revealed our secrets. "I'm just…he always acted so hateful to Tyler."

And there was where things got sticky. I did my best to explain how Felix and I had grown so close, without divulging his family situation. We sat there for easily fifteen minutes as I poured out the entire Soren and Felix BL romance manga come to life. When I ran out of words, she rubbed her eyes, then wrapped me in a big hug. She smelled of mango body mist. I held her to me, ignoring the looks from a couple of kids hustling by.

"I'm sorry for jumping all over you," she said, then pulled back to look me in the face. Her cheeks were damp. "And I totally get why you two are keeping it secret. I promise, I will not say a word to anyone. But next time, please have enough faith in me to tell me things."

"I do! I have all the faith in you, I just…it's been weird. I had to sort through my own shit, you know? How could I find this dude so hot when he was such a total asshole? We kind of…well, we worked things out. He's been through some shit, Court, like major life shit."

"Yeah, I know his dad had a heart attack." She patted at her cheeks to dry them as I left my arm around her shoulders.

"That was just one thing. There's other shit going on that I can't talk about because he told me in confidence. But he is coming around. He's like a different guy when we're together."

She smiled a wobbly smile. "You and Felix. It's

just…wow." She mimed explosions at her temples. I snickered a bit. "Still, I'll accept it as long as he treats you well. If he starts being an ass again, you let me know. I will chop him like firewood."

The girl was lethal with a field hockey stick. I'd seen her play, so I had no doubt she would crack shins when needed.

"Are you mad at me?" I had to ask.

She shook her head. "No. I was never mad." I cocked an eyebrow. "Okay, I was mad, but I was super confused and hurt. Now I get it. And when he's ready to come out, I will support him. He still has some work to do on his whole decent human being thing, but if he's trying, then I'll give him some space to rehab his asshole status."

"You're a good friend." I squeezed her tightly.

"You know it. Now let's get inside before my titties freeze and fall off."

She was *such* a summer girl.

---

THREE DAYS LATER, THE TEAM WAS GATHERED ON THE ice listening to my dad.

It was kind of surreal at times being the son of a legend. Like, people tried to befriend me just to get to

Tennant. Which sucked. A few of them had succeeded when I'd first been adopted, but I'd quickly learned to look for the warning signs. Now, my friends were *my* friends, and while they might be starstruck at first, they got over it quickly. Ten was only a dad after that initial starstruck moment.

"… always remember that no matter what you strive for in life—be it hockey or being a doctor or ranching or being an artist—go into that with determination to be the very best you can be. If you're working with pigs, then be the best pig farmer you can possibly be. If you're going to pursue the dream of being a pro athlete, then make sure you hit that ice and give a hundred percent every time. My brothers and I…"

I faded a bit as Ten spoke to the teens all kneeling around him. Not that my dad wasn't motivational, but I had heard these words, or similar ones before. Trust me. When you lived with two hockey players, every meal was peppered with Herb Brooks quotes. So while Ten was giving his rah-rah talk, my attention drifted to Felix. The way his hair curled around his ears, the various shades of blue in his eyes, the strong shape of his jaw, the length of his neck. I was really addicted to him. He sensed me gawking and gave me a shy peek that did funny things to me. My dick started to wake up. Not wanting to get hard while wearing a cup, I had to pull my attention from him. When I returned to my father, standing in the circle of eager young hockey players, Ten was talking, but his gaze was locked on me.

Knowing I'd been seen making eyes at Felix, I ducked my head to stare at my laces. The talk ended, and a small hands-on seminar took place with Ten showing us some of his tricks on the ice. How to lure a goalie to one side, then deke to the other. How to use your head to fool a tendie, things of that nature. All valuable hockey tips for sure, but my head was somewhere else. I'd made up my mind to ask Felix to the dance. Maybe. Shit. How could I do that? *Ugh.*

I waffled back and forth all the way through my shower. When I met Ten in the parking lot, the sun was setting, the sky clear as a bell.

"First thing Gramps will say when we get home is something about frost on the pumpkin," Dad said as we loaded my gear into his SUV.

"Probably," I replied. The frosty pumpkin had been a topic of conversation for a week now with my Gramps. Guess cold pumpkins were big news in the over-sixty set.

I sunk into the leather seat, tired and confused and horny, trying to take part in the chit-chat with my dad as we drove home. He reminded me that they were heading to Buffalo for one night, but would be back for Halloween, which was big news for Milo and Lottie. Everyone was going full Mandalorian this year, Lottie being Baby Yoda and Milo dressing up as Din Djarin. The two dads were Boba Fett and Moff Gideon. Our house was nerd central. And I lived for it all. So while they'd be out trick-or-treating, I'd either be at the dance alone, at the dance with Felix, or sitting at home sulking handing out Snickers. Man, this whole dating a closeted guy was rough. Worth it, but rough.

"… after dinner?" Ten asked when we pulled into our drive and he cut the engine.

"Sure, yeah." I had no clue, but I was sure it couldn't be anything too bad. Probably, just a reminder to take out the trash. Yep, life at the Rowe-Madsen house was pure glam.

Milo met us at the door, lower lip wobbly. I took over, rubbing his head, then leading him to the living room for a sit. He seemed to respond to me quicker than anyone else when he was anxious.

"What's up bud?" I asked, wiggling free of my jacket, then kicking off my Vans.

"I have a report to write about our family and…" He stalled, worried gaze scanning the area, then coming back to me. "Do they mean our new family, the old families we had, or our real mom family?"

Yikes. Yeah, I could see the confusion for him. I patted the couch, and he leapt onto it, burrowing into my side as he always did when he was upset. I rubbed his back as he chewed on his thumbnail. A step up from sucking it as he did when he was younger and stressed, but still tough on the cuticles.

"I bet they mean our new family. Which, you know, is our one true family. Like, legally and emotionally. Our dads are our dads, and the temporary families that we had before were just guardians until the right couple came along. Kind of like how Din Djarin was orphaned and raised by Mandalorians. He and us were foundlings who were rescued by super cool fighters. Only our heroes have skates, instead of jetpacks."

"Jetpacks are really cool," he whispered around his thumb.

"Totally," I concurred, then gave his hair a ruffle. That turned into a wrestling match that I let him win, just to see him smile.

We ate with the grandparents, Gramps talking about cold cucurbits, Grandma asking if I had practiced at the piano lately, while serving us her to-die-for tuna noodle casserole.

"No, not lately," I answered as Lottie picked out her peas, then tried to feed them to Gordie on the sly. "I promise I will over the weekend."

"Good. I know it seems silly, but if hockey doesn't work out, you'll have other skills to fall back on. You know that only one in four thousand players makes it to the NHL, so it's wise to have several back-ups for your future," Grandma said while I got weird looks from Ten and Jared.

"I'm going to be a Jedi when I grow up," Milo announced between slurping noodles into his mouth.

"I'm going to be a Jedi, too," Lottie announced, right as the dog stole her spoon and ran off with it. She began to cry, the dog whined and brought the spoon back and placed it on her lap, and Gramps got up to get Lottie a clean spoon. Dinner with the fam never disappointed.

After the trash run and helping sweep the kitchen, I went to my room to study and mope a bit more. Maybe mope wasn't the right word. I wasn't sad. Well, I kind of was. There was this burning need to be with Felix. Proudly be with him. As a couple. I thought we were couple-bound. Maybe, we were already there. It seemed like we could be if—

A soft rap at my door pulled my sight from the Chinese homework assignment I was not doing.

"Yeah," I called and both dads slipped inside, both looking as if they had gas. I'd not noticed tuna noodle being a large flatulence-producing meal, but then again, they *were* kind of old. Maybe peas did it? I knew Jared got all kinds of smelly when he ate raw broccoli.

"Hey, can we visit for a bit?" Jared asked.

I nodded, rolling to my side, then sitting up as they closed the door, then sat on my bed with me, one on each side.

"Did I do anything wrong?" I asked right off, a small kernel of worry they would say they were tired of me flaring to life. Stupid, yeah, and we were all legally family now, but old habits die hard.

"No, of course not," Jared said, his gaze dropping to my Chinese work, to Ten, then back to me. "Not at all. We're just... well, Tennant said he thought you were acting distracted during his team visit this afternoon."

I glanced at Ten.

"No, no, I did not say that. Exactly." Ten hurried to explain. "I just, well, I noticed that you and Felix Maxwell-Sinclair were shooting glances at each other. And I sensed that maybe it was time for me and your dad to sit down with you and have a talk."

Oh. Oh no. Oh please no. "Uhm, what kind of talk?"

"Well, the talk about sex," Jared said, and I felt an overwhelming need to crawl under my bed. "Now, we know you're sixteen. And that you feel that you know all about things of an intimate nature, and we're sure you know more than we did at your age."

"Speak for yourself," Ten muttered. Jared threw him a look. "What? I knew all about what tab went into what slot when I was like ten. I had two older brothers. Also, it wasn't like when *you* were a kid and had to get your news from the town crier."

A choked laugh escaped me. Jared sighed as Ten gave me a sly wink. "Anyway," Jared continued. "We wanted to make sure that you knew that you could come to us with any questions. We have no plans on pulling out diagrams—"

"Thank God," I said and got a smile from them both.

"We just wanted you to know that we're here. If you have any questions about any of it. Het sex, gay sex. Whatever. Also, and this is pretty important, we're happy to provide you with condoms if you are sexually active." Ten pulled up a leg to angle himself to face me better. "I know it can be embarrassing to go strolling into Hennessey's Pharmacy and ask for Trojans and lube."

I could feel my face growing hot. I had totally tried to do that just last week. And failed. Miserably. No way was I walking up to old man Hennessey and laying a box of Skyns and a tube of Astroglide down by the register. I'd sooner jerk off forever. No, that was a lie. I'd really rather not.

"He might not need lube if he dates a girl," Jared kindly pointed out. "But I guess it depends on what they're doing."

*Kill me now.*

Ten continued. "Sure, okay, but the looks that I saw flying between him and Felix kind of suggested that he's interested in a guy right now. And if he is, then eventually, they'll want to experiment and will need some lube to—"

"Okay, hey, wow, this has been amazingly informative, and I love that you guys are so cool about everything, but if we talk any more about butt stuff, I am going to slither under my bed to live among the dust bunnies forever."

They both stared at me for a moment, blushed, and got to their feet. "Cool, we get it. Just remember that we're here if you need anything, or just wish to talk. Our door is always open to you, son." Jared reached out to pat my cheek gently before he and Ten, who gave me a rock-on gesture, left me to myself.

Falling back on the bed, cheeks still warm, I chuckled at my life as my phone chirruped. I dug it out from under my ass and felt that familiar rush of emotion when I saw it was Felix calling.

I hurried to take the call on my laptop, eager to see his pretty blue eyes. When he did appear, I had a moment. Like a totally stupid and moronic moment. Getting to see him smiling at me made my brain sluggish. Probably due to all the blood above my belt rushing southward. Before he could even say hello, I blathered out ten words I'd not intended to blather.

"Would you like to go to the dance with me?"

## Chapter Eighteen

### Felix

THERE HAD BEEN A FEW TIMES IN MY LIFE WHERE MY world turned upside down, and inside out, but nothing that made my heart expand so big in my chest that I thought it might explode.

"You don't have to answer now," Soren said almost as quickly as he'd asked me.

Soren asking me to a dance was a different kind of upside down because it wasn't simply saying yes or no. It was coming out to the entire school, it was fingers pointing, and people talking shit, and leaving myself entirely open to being hurt. It was telling Dad, who was still not a hundred percent, and then, fitting the fact that I'm gay into whatever our new family life was going to be like.

Soren was so hopeful, his lips curved in a smile, and his expression would just become understanding if I said no because that was the kind of person he was. He could take a no and not have it undermine his entire life.

I could say no.

I had so much in my head that maybe I should say no.

"Yes," I blurted.

Soren's smile widened, and the screen moved as he fist-pumped before he grew serious. "We should talk about it though."

"Nope. No. Not doing that," I said. "No talking, no thinking. This isn't big. This isn't huge. This is just me going to a dance with someone I like a lot, and… yeah."

"You like me?" Soren whispered and leaned into the phone so he was all blurry. "Or do you *like me*."

"Don't push it Rowe," I snarked.

Soren fell back on his pillow. "Whatever, Sinclair," he grinned. Then, he got serious. "How's your dad? I should have asked that first."

"He's grumpy that he has to take it easy, but yeah, he's good."

"Good," Soren repeated, then went very quiet, and part of me considered that he was about to retract his offer about the dance. My belly held a bucket of butterflies, and it hit me how shit it would be if he told me he was joking, or that he'd changed his mind. I deserved it after how messed up I'd been in some of the things I said to him.

"I'm sorry," I blurted. "I really like your dads, and I'm sorry for the things I said to you about them."

He frowned, and I wished I'd just kept my mouth shut.

"I know," he said simply. "I wouldn't have asked you to the dance if I didn't know that."

"Oh."

"I was going to ask, and you don't have to, because this is a big family thing, and I think my stepbrother is going to be there as well, and you haven't met him but…"

"Ryker, he plays for Arizona."

"Yeah, he's cool, but look… it's my birthday in two days. Would you like to come over to, like, this party thing the 'rents have going on? It's going to be a ton of family, and starts at two, and they said I could invite whoever, and I have. I mean Tyler will be there, and, obviously, Court and everyone, y'know. I'm going to text the team, but before I did that, I wanted to personally invite *you*, so you don't think you're just part of a group chat or something."

He seemed unsure of himself, as if this was a harder question to ask than getting me to the Halloween dance.

"Felix?" he prompted, and I didn't have to be an expert to know I was messing things up by not answering immediately.

"Of course. I'd love to," I said quickly. "I was just thinking what to get you for a gift."

"Just yourself and, maybe, a kiss?" he asked with hope.

"I can do that."

We both got quiet then, as if we were all out of emotions that didn't involve grinning like idiots. A quick goodnight, and then, I hugged my screen to my chest and screwed my eyes shut. I was so excited, and nervous, and happy, and… I didn't know what to do with the emotions, and also, I was so damn hungry. I placed the screen carefully on my desk, squared it up to the corner, then stared at it for a long time. I wondered what Soren was doing now; was he as excited as me? Was he nervous? My stomach grumbled, reminding me that I'd already decided a midnight snack run was priority—not that it was midnight, but any time after ten seemed as if it counted. I headed to the kitchen and flicked on the light, the counter illuminated, and my dad blinking at me as he'd been sitting in the dark for some grown-up reason. I think I understood what it was when I glanced at all the property details strewn in front of him.

"Hey son," Dad said, shuffling the prints into a neat pile. "I'll get out of your way."

"It's okay, Dad, I just wanted to get a snack."

"Phoebe left pie if you want to heat it up. There's ice cream there as well." He glanced at me with a hopeful expression.

"Is that you saying that you want some pie?" I deadpanned.

His lips curved into a smile. "Well, I wouldn't want you eating on your own, and what my dietician doesn't know about won't hurt her."

I cut two pieces of pie, his smaller, nuked them, fetched the ice cream and forks, and placed one in front of Dad, and then, taking the stool on the opposite side of the counter, reached for the top property details. "Is this one of the potential houses you're looking at?" I glanced at the paper as I shoveled in the first mouthful of apple and pastry. The place seemed nice enough, smaller than here, but if it was just Dad and me, and then, just Dad when I left for college, it was great.

"Yeah. It's hard to decide what to do for the best given I grew to like this place."

"You mean despite it being Mom's idea to buy it?" I huffed at that, but Dad glanced at me and seemed pained.

"I'm not going to talk bad about your mom, Felix. After all, she gave me you, and I love you." He dipped his gaze and his cheeks flushed red. He was actually embarrassed to allow me to see that part of him, and it hurt.

"I love you too, Dad," I responded, and he smiled at me. "Can we talk for a minute?"

"Isn't that what we're doing?" He seemed puzzled as he ate a mouthful of pie.

"I mean talk about important stuff."

He paused eating and placed his fork on the plate. "Sure. I know divorce is hard on kids, and if there's anything I can do to stop you worrying, we could—"

"I'm gay, Dad." I blurted, and he blinked at me the same as when I'd turned the lights on, as if he couldn't focus on my face. "I've known for a while now, but it's been buried, like super buried, way down, but I met someone, and he's…"

"He's what?" Dad prompted.

"He's just perfect. For me, I mean. No, he's actually pretty perfect all together."

"Is it someone from school?"

Was I ready to share Soren's name? Well, I guess he would find out sooner, rather than later. *Here goes nothing.* "It's Soren. Soren Madsen-Rowe."

Dad stared at me, and for a horrible dark moment, I expected a lecture, and couldn't imagine the pain Mom would be heaping on me right now for this *decision*.

"How long have you known you were gay?" Dad asked cautiously.

"A few years now; I don't know exactly." Where was this going?

"Is it my fault?" Dad asked, and my whole world slipped again, only this time, it was a disappointment so big I couldn't even see the edges of it. Was he saying he'd somehow turned me gay? What the actual fuck!

"I was born gay, Dad!" I shouted, and he was instantly horrified.

"No! Wait, of course you were," he said, "Jeez, I'm doing this wrong." He pushed back his stool, and it clattered into the stove. Then, he hurried around the counter and opened his arms. "What I meant was, I'm sorry that I was a shit dad and you couldn't tell me before. It's my fault, and I'm so sorry." I took a moment to process everything—he wasn't saying he'd made me gay; he was saying that he thought I'd kept it a secret from him because of who we'd become to each other. I rose into a real dad/son hug, and he held me tight, and then, stood me away from him. "I'm so proud of you," he said, his eyes bright with emotion. "I like Soren a lot. I guess I should have a chat with his dads, and wait..." He glanced around the kitchen. "I have condoms, but do we have any bananas? I need to give you a talk."

"You're not giving me the talk," I grinned at him, and then fake-punched his arm.

He hugged me again. "I love you, Felix. I love that you told me."

And I loved him for loving me, and the person I was becoming.

But more than that, I loved that we didn't have any bananas.

———

ARRIVING AT SOREN'S HOUSE WAS LIKE WALKING INTO hockey central. I recognized so many of the guys from the Harrisburg Railers standing around chatting, and I managed to avoid talking to any of them as I sidled to the edge and made it to where Tyler was.

"Hey," I said, and he jumped so high that soda spilled, and he yelped. "Sorry, I thought you saw me coming," I apologized.

He winced. "Yeah," was all he said, and seemed to retreat further into the alcove he'd found between one trophy cabinet and the next. Neither of which held trophies, or if they did, then they were hidden behind photographs of Soren, Milo, and Lottie, plus the winger from the Arizona Raptors—Ryker— Soren's stepbrother through their dad Jared. It must be cool to have siblings—adopted or otherwise—and to have actual stars connected to you must be beyond cool.

"You seen Soren?" I asked Tyler, who shook his head and shrunk a little further when a couple of the big hockey players let out bellowing laughs and stumbled back to encroach in our space. I didn't know what was happening here, but I put an arm over Tyler's shoulder and encouraged him out through the crowd and into the back yard, straight over to where I could see Milo and Lottie with a curly-haired guy who had his back to us. The three of them were digging in a sandpit, building a huge castle festooned with tiny flags, and as soon as we reached them, Tyler relaxed as if the weight of something had slipped from his shoulders. The guy there, the one with the curly hair, was none other than out and pretty NHL star, Ryker, Soren's oldest sibling. The only drawback about him was that he played for a team I didn't follow, but I knew him, and when he smiled at us, it was like looking at sunshine.

"Hey, Tyler," sunshine-Ryker said, and exchanged fist bumps before Tyler went to a crouch to work on the castle. "Hey…"

"Felix," I answered and extended a hand to shake.

Ryker's eyes widened, then he took my hand and pulled me in a side hug. "Halloween dance guy," he announced and scanned the yard. "Soren!" he called.

I spotted Soren jogging up the vast lawn with a wide grin. He came to a sliding stop in front of me.

"Hey," he said shyly, then pulled me into a hug.

"Happy belated birthday party," I whispered in his ear, and the hug went on and on. I inhaled the scent of him—a mix of body spray and the outside—and wanted the hug to last forever, but it couldn't, and then, I was being held close, standing opposite his stepbrother who watched us carefully. Did Ryker know what an ass I'd been? Did he realize I was still a work in progress? Did he know I'd hit Tyler, and that I'd tried to make Soren's life miserable? Did he know what I'd said about his dads?

Ryker shoved at Soren. "Go away and say a proper happy birthday," he said, and went back to playing with sand, only then, he glanced up. "Did Dad give you the talk?"

"What talk?" Lottie asked and stared up at us.

"Nothing, Lottie," Ryker immediately said and covered her ears. "Did he?"

"Yeah," Soren said, and he and Ryker snorted a laugh. "Hey, at least you just got your dad; I got both of them. It was mortifying."

We started to walk away. "I do have a gift to give you," I murmured. "It's not much, but I know that your favorite hockey player is—"

"Not here, come with me. I've got something to show you." He took my hand and threaded his way past family and friends, stopping every so often to talk, with me right by his side, and every time he introduced me as his boyfriend, not one person batted an eyelid. In fact, I got hugs and hellos, and the feeling grew that they were all wrong because they didn't know the real *me*. I attempted to tug my hand free of Soren's, but he was holding so tight, caught up in the love and smiles from family and friends, where all I felt was a need to escape. Just when I thought I might tackle him to the ground, he pulled me through a gate and out to the garages, and I was never more relieved than when it shut behind us and all the madness was contained. I bent at the waist, getting myself together, and after a moment, Soren peered up and under at my face.

"You okay?"

"Do they all know what I said? Do they know what I did?"

He glanced at the gate, then back again. "No. Only my dads, and they get it."

"Get what?"

Soren shrugged. "Being a kid. Life."

That was such a simple answer to the most complicated of equations, and somehow it made sense, but it didn't let me off the hook. Instead, it made me want to be a better person, to take this life I'd been messing up and make it different. Soren made me want to be better, and I wanted to deserve his trust.

"Anyway, look!" Soren said and gestured at the driveway. "My car."

I'd imagined a brand-new car, with a big scarlet bow, the same thing Mom had sent me, which sat in the garage untouched, right next to my dad's Mercedes, which he said I could drive whenever I wanted. Instead, I saw a later model Prius in pale blue, no custom plates, no bow, and scratched in places.

"Isn't she beautiful?" He tugged me over and petted the hood. "My dads matched every dollar I saved from chores, babysitting, and yard work, that kind of thing, and then, with all my birthday money added to the pot, I managed to find enough to buy her from a friend of theirs. What do you think?"

What did I think of the older, but probably very sensible and safe Prius? I thought it had been earned with love and affection, and I loved everything about it. I craved that, and I wanted to whoop with Soren, and love on the damn car, and then, cry. I tugged my hand from his.

"I need to apologize to your dads, to Tyler, to Jonah and Courtney. I need to hug my dad, and I'm sorry, I just need to…"

He hurried after me as I ran through the gate and headed to where I'd last seen Soren's parents, finding them in a group of men with kids, and I pushed my way in—not a good start, but I didn't know how else to do this. I was usually so full of defensiveness and hate that gave me bravery, but this was stripped down.

"I'm sorry," I blurted to Ten, who was smiling at me and, then, at Soren, who reached me and gripped my hand as if he'd never let it go. "I'm sorry I used the F-word; I'm sorry I said you went dumpster diving for kids."

"You said what now?" Someone asked, and I went scarlet.

"I'm sorry I was so messed up and horrible and…" My breathing hitched, and then, stopped when Tennant *freaking* Madsen-Rowe pulled me in for a hug and held me tight.

"It's all good," he murmured. "You can breathe now."

And actually, it felt like I could.

---

SOREN AND I SAT IN THE PRIUS AFTER EVERYONE HAD left, and it seemed as if we were in the middle of an amazing adventure, even just sitting there and staring at the garage beyond. The possibilities were endless: a space to talk, to drive when he could, to get ourselves away from anyone who could see us. The only small issue was that Tyler and Courtney were in the back seat rummaging through a box of CDs they'd found under my seat. The fact that Soren had asked me to sit up front with him, for this inaugural sitting and going nowhere thing, was pretty cool.

I felt different. *Special*.

"So my present?" Soren teased, and I blinked at him as I realized I hadn't yet given him his present. It wasn't much, but I'd dug into my escape fund and got him the best thing I could find. I dug into my jacket and pulled out the small, wrapped gift, and he turned it over in his hands and rattled it, even though it was obviously a card of some sort.

"You'll probably be super disappointed—"

"No, I won't." He leaned over and kissed me, much to Tyler and Courtney's amusement, and then, he unwrapped it, opening a signed card featuring Xander Holden, the captain of the Boston Rebels, the first out hockey-playing captain of a team.

"I know you're not a Boston fan, but I remember you doing that speech in English about your hero, and this was what—oomph."

He kissed me again, cradling my face awkwardly and kissing me hard, and when we separated, we were both grinning.

All four of us had cake in napkins, and there were two huge bowls of chips—one for us in the front, one for them in the back. The sodas were cold, the car was warm, and the same as most of the day, Soren was holding my hand, our fingers laced, and I had to get home in a bit, but for now, I was living the dream.

# Epilogue

## Soren

"How did you manage to get this shirt so wrinkled?" Grandma asked, holding the light pink dress shirt up by its collar. "It looks like you wadded it up into a ball, then slam-dunked it into the hamper."

"It kind of just fell off the hanger a few days ago in the closet, and I didn't see it." I gave her my saddest puppy dog eyes. "Can you iron it for me?"

She smiled. "No." I gaped at her. "I can show *you* how to iron it yourself. There's no reason a man cannot do his own ironing. Come along."

I threw a glance at my grandfather. He peeked over the top of the paper he was scanning, reading glasses on the tip of his nose. Milo and Lottie were engrossed in *The Muppet Show*, the variety show from the late seventies and early eighties. I kind of liked it myself. Animal was the man.

"She's right. All our boys know how to cook, sew, iron, and pay the bills," Gramps said in commiseration. "I do as well. The sewing was a dicey learning experience, but I now have great skills in reattaching buttons. Anything else goes to my lovely wife."

"Sweet talker. Come along, let's get the iron out," Grandma said, leading me to the laundry room where, lo and behold, an ironing board hung on pegs on the wall. It was a little dusty. "My stars, do your fathers never iron?"

"Not really. I think it's like a thing from ye olden days," I commented as I hoisted myself up onto the washer to watch how this worked. Grandma gave me an eye roll. "I think it really is. No one I know irons."

"Well, there are some skills that everyone should know. How to press off a dress shirt is one of them." She handed me my shirt, flipped open the ironing board with ninja-like skills, then reached up over the washer/dryer to pluck the iron from the shelf. That too was covered with dust. "What if you have a job interview and need to look tidy?"

"Most of those are done online," I replied,

watching with little interest as she plugged in the iron before glancing at me. "What? They are. But I get what you're saying."

"Good. All young men need to know how to take care of themselves. You can't expect your wife or husband to coddle you like your mother did." Her eyes rounded. "I'm sorry. That was…I wasn't thinking and just trotted out the lines I used on my boys."

"It's cool." She looked stricken. "No, really, it's cool. I know what you're saying, and I get it. Both sexes need to know how to do domestic things."

"That's right." Her tiny hand gave my knee a quick squeeze, then she showed me the iron settings and which ones to use. Nodding along, I watched her position my pink shirt then slowly begin pressing the wrinkles out of it with a very hot iron. "Just like being prepared for a career after hockey is important."

"I'm not really sure I'm going to go into hockey," I commented as the smell of warm cotton reached my nose. She threw me a surprised look, but kept moving the iron. "I know everyone thinks I will because of who my dads are, but I'm thinking of counseling. Maybe working with social services, and other kids like me and Milo."

She lifted the iron from the back of my shirt, her

eyes filled with tears. Oh great, I made my grandmother cry the night of the Halloween dance. The night I was going to walk into the Chesterford auditorium with Felix holding my hand. The biggest night of our lives. And I made my grandmother cry. What kind of shitty person was I?

"That's a wonderful vocation, Soren. Simply wonderful." Oh. Okay, so they were happy tears. Cool. Phew. She sniffled, then went back to ironing. "You have such a kind and empathetic nature. Look at the wonders you worked with Felix."

"I think Felix did all that work on himself, *by* himself."

"Oh, I'm not so sure." She flipped the shirt around to press a crinkled sleeve. "Without you as a guiding star, he might not have ever seen the errors of his ways. A true and good friend can always help guide you down a better path. I think you're selling yourself short."

I wasn't so convinced about all of that, but it was nice to hear. She gave me a loving little smile, then started talking about spray starch. Not a clue what that was, but she seemed to think it was something pretty amazing. Once my shirt was pressed, I rushed upstairs to shower, shave off the dark whiskers on my chin, and pull on my suit. I did a spin in front of the mirror on my door, examining myself from every angle. Yeah, I was a stud. Felix was going to be so hot for me.

FUNNY THING. WHEN I SAW FELIX IN HIS DARK BLUE suit, it was *me* who was so hot for *him*. The man was gorgeous.

Honestly, he was the prettiest boy in Pennsylvania. Anyone who felt otherwise could come at me. We met at the school, my grandmother escorting us to the door so she could take about ten thousand pictures to send to my dads who were in Canada for a road trip. That was one of the biggest downsides to having a pro hockey player as a parent. The travel. They missed so many important things. Things, I knew, they both wanted to be here for, which sucked for them as much—or maybe even more—than it did for me, Milo, and Lottie.

"Oh, why does it keep beeping at me?" Grandma asked in confusion-slash-frustration.

"Hold on," I laughed, then darted over to get her phone camera set up for her. This was a daily thing with the grand folks. It was either their laptop or their phone or their desktop that wasn't working right. In truth, it was usually them who weren't working right, but I wouldn't say that to them. "Okay, so when you bring up your camera you don't have to hold it so long. Just snap the picture like on an old camera. No, no, that's... no, that's editing, no, now you're trying to crop the image. Nope, okay, here let me have it for a second."

She handed it over, staring up at me as if I hung the moon and the stars. Honestly, having a grandma and gramps was the best thing ever. It was right up there with having two dads, a sibling, two step-siblings, and a bunch of cool friends. Oh, and a boyfriend. A pretty boyfriend. Prettiest boy in the state. Fight me.

"There it's all set to go. Now, when you see us, just tap the little circle." I gave her a quick hug, then darted back to Felix. She'd positioned us under an oak tree the student council had hung with little tissue ghosts. No one was in costume. Chesterford didn't do that kind of dance. They did semiformal, corporate casual, and formal for the proms. Felix looked a little tight, but he smiled through the million snapshots.

"You two are so handsome," Grandma said after sending the pictures to my dads and the Rowe family chat, which took forever due to how many people were in that chat. I had cousins all over the place, girls mostly, from Florida to Boston, as well as Ryker and his husband out west, *and* all the Railers who for some reason got images of me at a school dance. Why? Not a clue, but that was how the Railers team worked. Family. It was really pretty damn neat. "Okay, so your grandfather will be here at eleven to pick you both up. He likes driving in the dark more than I do. I hate those big bold headlights on some people's cars. Honestly, are they trying to see to the next county?"

I smiled. Felix smiled. Kids arriving for the dance raced past, breath fogging in front of them, most hand in hand. How Halloween could be a romantic setting for a dance, I had no clue, but I could already hear some pretty good tunes flowing out into the chilly night every time someone entered.

We waved at my grandmother as she headed back to her car, standing side by side under the haunted oak tree, and then, I turned to him.

"Are you okay?" I asked, shoulders rising up to my ears as a brisk fall wind shook the tiny ghosts overhead. "We don't have to do this." He made a face. "No, I'm serious. We do not have to go in and be all 'Look at us we're a couple!' if you're not ready. We can totally skip this dance and go to Hot Pot Noodle Shop for some killer ramen."

"You're being really nice," Felix said. "But I want

to do this. I do. I swear. It's just…I'm nervous. I was a dick to people for so long, making stupid jokes and—"

I placed my index finger over his lips. "You've changed. People see it. Hey, we all say and do stupid shit when we're scared and trying to protect ourselves. I get it. Others do too. They will accept the new you once they see you being super cute and cool day in and day out. Also, just saying, you do have *the* sexiest mother-humper in the whole school as your date. That will impress the hell out of all of them. They'll all be thinking that if Soren Madsen-Rowe is with this dude, he must be epic." He rolled his eyes so hard it was a wonder they didn't pop out of his head and roll down into the storm drain a few feet away. "I'm just saying that whatever you want to do here is your call. I'm with you no matter what." I took his hand, kissed his knuckles, then stood there freezing my balls off while he stared at me for what seemed like hours.

"Let's do this." He turned and tramped up the stairs, my fingers death-gripped in his. As soon as the doors were pulled open, we were nearly blasted back outside by the sheer volume of *Goo Goo Muck* by The Cramps as everyone in the student body—and several staff chaperones—broke into the Wednesday dance. Lights moved around the dance floor, smoke crawled along the parquet, and the spooky giant paper trees in the corners swayed as fans blew over the dancers. The school really went all out for their dances, not going to lie. The DJ was worth whatever they were paying him. He, then, eased right into *Howlin' for You* by The Black Keys, a song I knew well as it was one that was on every playlist Ten possessed.

Felix pulled me right into the thick of things as the song kicked into something slower. People gawked at us, many leaning in to whisper to each other and their friends. We stood there in the middle of the smoke and roaming lights, staring at one another, his hand in mine. I was going to let him lead on this, as it was his announcement to make or not however he wished. Some old song began to play, one I'd never heard before with some dude singing about come hither stares and witchcraft. Which kind of worked because I was spellbound by Felix for sure.

He didn't say a word. He leaned in to place his lips to mine. I sighed into the kiss, moving in to slip my arms around his lean frame. Talk about making a statement.

When we pulled apart, his cheeks were flushed and his eyes glowing. Courtney, Tyler, and the rest of our friends and teammates flowed out of the dancers to hug us both in a show of support and acceptance of Felix, me, and every other queer kid who took that giant step to show the world just who they were deep down inside. He was brave, and he was mine.

"You're amazing," I shouted to be heard over the hoots when the DJ fired up *Monster* by Lady Gaga. Old, sure, but a solid dance beat. "Want to dance?"

He nodded, smiling as wide as I had ever seen a person smile.

"I'm not a good dancer," he yelled back.

"I'll still like you anyway."

"I'll still like you too. A lot!" He bellowed, then broke out some truly interesting dance moves. Yeah, for sure, he was the prettiest boy here, and my heart was his.

Even if he did have two left feet.

THE END

What's next for the Chesterford
Coyotes?
_____

*On Thin Ice (Fall 2023)*

**A young adult hockey romance filled with making
amends, family, friends, and discovering the real
person inside while juggling the crazy, upside-
down world of high school.**

Jonah Robinson has really messed up and making
amends isn't going to be easy when people label him
as the bad boy of Chesterford Academy. With the help
of his family and a special friend at the school, Jonah
is determined to make things right with those he
wronged. The first person on that long redemption list
is Tyler, the brightest player on the Coyotes, at least
in Jonah's eyes. He's taken a thousand pictures of
Tyler for the school paper, but he's going to have to

learn how to develop more than just negatives if he wants to grow close to Tyler.

Tyler Corrigan's dad has left, his mom is terrified he'll come back, and it's Tyler who's left to keep his little family in one piece. The only respite from real life is playing hockey, and he's an important part of the Chesterford Coyotes. Despite not being the biggest person on the ice, speed is his superpower, and the team has his back during the worst of the bullying he's had to endure. His friends make him feel safe when his real world is full of fear, but no one can protect his heart when an awkward and messed up Jonah—one of the most confusing of his bullies—is suddenly around every corner, wanting to make things right.

Sorry can be impossible to believe, but trusting your heart is everything.

---

Sign up here for reminders

mmhockeyromance.com/YANL

## Hockey from Scott & Locey

### Harrisburg Railers (Hockey Romance)

Changing Lines | First Season | Deep Edge | Poke Check | Last Defense | Goal Line | Neutral Zone | Hat Trick | Save The Date | Baby Makes Three | Rivals

*Railers Volume 1 | Railers Volume 2 | Railers Volume 3*

### Owatonna U Hockey (Hockey Romance)

Ryker | Scott | Benoit | Christmas Lights | Valentine's Hearts | Desert Dreams

### Arizona Raptors (Hockey Romance)

Coast To Coast | Across the Pond | Shadow and Light | Sugar and Ice | School and Rock

### Boston Rebels

Lost In Boston (Free Novella) | Top Shelf | Back Check | Snowed | Royal Lines | Blade | Rental

# LA Storm

*Script (August 2023)| Savage | Symbol | Spades | Second | Styled*

## Chesterford Coyotes - Young Adult Romance

*Off the Ice | On Thin Ice*

## Meet RJ Scott

RJ discovered romance in books at a very young age and realized that if there wasn't romance on the page, she could create it in her head. With over one hundred and fifty books published, she is a full time author of gay romance.

She lives and works out of her home in the beautiful English countryside, spends her spare time reading, watching films, and enjoying time with her family.

The last time she had a week's break from writing she didn't like it one little bit and has yet to meet a box of chocolates she couldn't defeat.

www.rjscott.co.uk | rj@rjscott.co.uk

**NEWSLETTER - rjscott.co.uk/rjnews**

facebook.com/author.rjscott

x.com/Rjscott_author

instagram.com/rjscott_author

amazon.com/author/rj-scott

bookbub.com/authors/rj-scott

goodreads.com/rjscott

pinterest.com/rjscottauthor

## Meet V.L. Locey

V.L. Locey loves worn jeans, yoga, belly laughs, walking, reading and writing lusty tales, Greek mythology, the New York Rangers, comic books, and coffee.

(Not necessarily in that order.)

She shares her life with her husband, her daughter, one dog, two cats, a flock of assorted domestic fowl, and two Jersey steers.

When not writing spicy romances, she enjoys spending her day with her menagerie in the rolling hills of Pennsylvania with a cup of fresh java in hand.

vllocey.com
vicki@vllocey.com

Newsletter - vllocey.com/newsletter

facebook.com/V.L.Locey

x.com/vllocey

instagram.com/vl_locey

bookbub.com/authors/v-l-locey

goodreads.com/vllocey

pinterest.com/vllocey